A SOLDIER'S TRIUMPH

AN EAGLE SECURITY & PROTECTION AGENCY NOVEL, BEYOND VALOR 3

LYNNE ST. JAMES

A Soldier's Triumph

Copyright © 2017 by Lynne St. James
Cover Art Copyright © 2017 by Lynne St. James
Published by Coffee Bean Press
Cover Art by LoriJacksonDesign.com
Created in the United States

This book is a work of fiction. Names, characters, places and incidents are products of the author's imagination or used fictitiously. Any resemblance to actual events or locales or persons living or dead is entirely coincidental.

No part of this work may be used, stored, reproduced or transmitted without written permission from the publisher except for brief quotations for review purposes as permitted by law.

This book is licensed for your personal enjoyment only and may not be re-sold or given away to other people. If you would like to share this book, please purchase an additional copy for each person.

If you're reading this book and did not purchase it, or it was not purchased for your use only, please purchase your own copy. Thank you for respecting the hard work of this author.

If you find any of my eBooks being sold or shared illegally, please contact me at Lynne@LynneStJames.com.

✿ Created with Vellum

DEDICATION

*For all the spouses and families who are patiently
waiting for their soldier to come home.*

As always, for T.S. I love you!

A SOLDIER'S TRIUMPH

He might be broken, but he'd do anything to protect his wife.

Wounded in action, Alex Barrett is stuck in a wheelchair. But it won't stop him from protecting the love of his life. Come hell or high water, he'll find a way to keep Lily safe.

Devastated by how close she'd come to losing her husband, Lily Barrett will do anything to protect him—even if it means not telling him when her life is threatened.

Alex hopes to keep Lily safe with the help of his service dog, Hunter, and some old teammates who run the Eagle Security & Protection Agency. Will these ex-military men be able to help Alex save his wife before it's too late?

PROLOGUE

S*even months earlier…*

It had to be a nightmare. Except she couldn't make it stop. Even before the phone rang, she'd known. She'd been watching *Frozen* with Lexie and Bella for what had to be the fifteenth time in two days when she doubled over from a crushing pain in her chest. Sweat beaded on her forehead and an image of Alex lying in a pool of blood flashed in her mind.

As if she'd somehow summoned it, the phone vibrated on the coffee table. Staring at it with detached fascination, she couldn't move. Lexie looked at her then back to the phone.

"Aren't you going to answer it, Aunt Lily?"

The sound of the child's voice snapped her out of whatever fog she'd been in. "Yes, of course." The screen offered no answers. A blocked number. Dread churned in her stomach.

"Lily Barrett."

"Mrs. Barrett. Captain Durant here. I am sorry. I have to inform you that Alex has been wounded in action…" He continued to speak, but after he'd said Alex's name and wounded all she heard was blah, blah, blah. "Mrs. Barrett? Lily?" He must have asked her a question. What the hell was it? Searching her mind, hoping her sub-conscious could recall the words, she came up empty.

"I'm sorry. Can you repeat that?" Expecting impatience, she was surprised when he sounded almost fatherly.

"Alex has been seriously injured in an explosion. He's in surgery. That's all I know for now."

"All you know, or all you can tell me?"

The sigh traveled the thousands of miles very clearly. "I'm sorry. He's in surgery and as soon as there is more…"

It wasn't enough. They all knew it was standard procedure, but it didn't make it easier. "What am I supposed to do?"

"Right now, nothing, ma'am. You'll be contacted as soon as there's an update. I'm very sorry."

After taking a deep breath and forcing down the bile that threatened to spew from her mouth, she choked out the words, "thank you."

Without thinking she dialed Chloe. Her best friend and the mother of the two girls sitting on the couch staring at her like she'd grown a second head. Had she? Maybe she should check? She got up to look in the mirror in the front hall. Nope, only one head, but there were tears sliding down her cheeks. As if watching a movie, she reached up and slid her fingers through the wet trails. When did that happen? No wonder the girls were staring at her.

"Hello?"

"Chloe…oh my God…" It was all she could get out before the tears started in earnest. Gasping for breath, she doubled over from the pain squeezing her heart.

"Lily? What happened? Is it the girls? Are they hurt?"

Forcing herself to take slow breaths while trying to get control of the pain, she struggled to answer Chloe. "Why would you ask about the girls?" Lily checked, they were still watching *Frozen*. Why would she... Shit. "No, I mean yes. Fuck. They're fine. I'm sorry. I...I don't..."

"What's wrong? You're not making sense." Lily knew she wasn't, and she was trying her best to get her thoughts organized to force them out of her mouth. But it wasn't working. The sick feeling permeating her being had struck like a bolt of lightning. Hearing Captain Durant's voice only sealed the deal.

"Lily? What's going on?"

"It's Alex..." It was all she could get out.

"He's not..."

"Wounded in combat. I don't know what to do." She tried to hold it together, she did, but it was a losing battle. The girls didn't need to know what was going on it would only scare them. "Can your mom come and get the girls? I don't..."

"Of course. I'll call her now. We're coming home. I'll be there as soon as I can. He's tough, he'll be fine."

Lily nodded, then realized Chloe couldn't see it. "I hope so," she whispered, every word like a prayer. He needed to be okay. He was the love of her life, and she couldn't lose him.

"Lily?" No answer. The house was eerily silent as if no one was home, but Chloe knew her friend was there, if for no other reason than her car was in the driveway. She went from room to room until she found her lying on the bed curled into a ball hugging a stuffed teddy bear. She remembered it, it was the one Alex had brought home at Christmas. Lily clutched it like a lifeline.

"Sweetie, I'm here now. Can I get you anything?" She wasn't sure she'd get an answer. As she neared the side of the bed, she saw tears rolling down Lily's cheeks, but she wasn't making a sound. "Lily?"

"I'm okay."

"No, you're not, and that's okay. I'm not either. Please come back to my house. I don't think you should be alone."

"I can't leave. What if Alex comes home?" Chloe sucked in a breath. Not quite sure what to say.

"He won't be home tonight. He's in surgery, right? That's what you told me."

"But I have to wait for him. He might show up." Shock, denial, all the things they were told to be prepared for if the worst happened. Chloe sat on the edge of the bed and pulled Lily into a hug. They rocked back and forth their tears mingling for a long while.

When Lily's tears finally slowed, Chloe got up and packed her a bag. No way was Lily staying there by herself. She couldn't believe they didn't know more yet, even Logan, Chloe's husband Alex's best friend, hadn't been able to get any further information from the captain. Or if he had, he couldn't tell her. Sometimes being a military wife sucked donkey balls.

CHAPTER 1

P*resent Day…*

They'd been home a week, and Lily was already pulling her hair out. Alex had a long road ahead of him if she didn't kill him first. She'd thought what they'd gone through at Walter Reed was tough, but this was a thousand times worse. In the hospital, there'd been a buffer between her and his pain and moodiness. The doctors, volunteers, nurses, and therapists, had been in and out of his hospital room. Now that it was all on her, she was worried she couldn't be the woman, the support, the wall, he needed her to be for him.

Sheer terror and worry about losing him had morphed into the overwhelming joy that he'd survive and she wouldn't lose the man of her dreams. Since they'd met, somehow, she'd known he was her destiny. Not one to believe in love at first sight, she fought it, but eventually, they both gave in after they got past the friends to lovers' phase. And she'd never looked back.

The reality of his recovery and the agony he faced daily shredded her heart. If it hadn't been for her best friend, Chloe, she'd have lost it long before now. Even with a new baby and her young daughters, Lexie and Bella, she'd taken every one of Lily's calls. Listened to her as she sobbed her heart out for countless hours after leaving Walter Reed National Military Hospital every evening.

Not that the military hadn't offered tons of support. From being able to stay at the medical complex in one of the Fisher Houses, to the counseling and the comradery of the other families going through the same thing, it should have made things easier. Should being the operative word. Lily had never found it easy to share her feelings. She'd tried. It hadn't been easy, but by the time Alex was released, she'd made some new friends and helped a few other wives—at least she hoped she had.

Many of the other wives seemed so much stronger, and most even had children to deal with. Seeing their strength made her feel weak. So many tears she'd shed for the life they'd envisioned and now seemed lost. Her pain wasn't just for Alex either, which made her feel even worse. Her dreams of a family might have to be put away forever. All her focus needed to be on helping Alex, the rest didn't matter. But she wasn't going to lie to herself either. She was worried she wouldn't be strong enough to be his rock.

After three surgeries and countless hours of physical therapy, they told him he *should* be able to walk again—eventually—but not how painful the process would be. He'd been standing near the truck when the bomb exploded and been thrown over ten feet by the blast. Shrapnel had carved through his uniform and sliced into his body. Most of the pieces had been removed, and the cuts had healed. Lily didn't care about his new scars. As far as she was concerned, he was still the sexiest man in the world and no scar would change that. Too bad he didn't believe it. Besides being confined to a wheelchair for now, and she was convinced it was only 'for now,' the part of Alex that had been affected the most was his self-confidence.

Alex had always been the life of the party, it didn't matter if the jokes were politically correct or not, he was in it for the laughs and his friends knew it. He'd offended some along the way, but they realized most of the time the jokes were directed at himself. Now everything was changed because of a two-inch chunk of shrapnel resting against the edge of his spine. Surgery was too risky until the swelling went down, and how long it would take was anyone's guess. The doctors sure as shit didn't have a clue. That left Alex in pain and restricted to the wheelchair. It's not that he was paralyzed, he wasn't, and Lily thanked God for that. Although to listen to Alex he might as well be. The doctors insisted he needed to give it time and take it easy, but those words weren't in his vocabulary.

And that led them to now. She'd just stepped out of the shower when she heard it. *Damn it.* Last night she'd forgotten to put the mugs on the counter when she'd set up the coffee to auto-brew. It was the first time she'd forgotten since they'd gotten home. If the crash and yell were any indication, he'd tried to reach them on his own, and it hadn't ended well.

She was exhausted and overwhelmed, but it was no excuse. She needed to make sure he was taken care of and protected. Wrapping the towel around her, she ran down the stairs to the kitchen, praying he hadn't been burned by the scalding coffee or worse.

"What happened? Are you okay?" Her words trailed off as she saw Alex, in his wheelchair next to the kitchen counter. The floor surrounding him was covered with bits and pieces of porcelain. Thankfully, it was dry, so he hadn't gotten as far as the hot coffee and wasn't burned.

"I fucked up. I was trying to get a damn cup of coffee. Instead, I managed to create another mess for you to deal with. I'm a waste product now, I tell you."

"It's just a mug," she said as she took a deep breath and tried to calm her racing heart. She meant it. It was a coffee cup. They could buy hundreds more. But Alex? He could never be replaced. Why couldn't he see it?

"I wanted a cup of coffee without having to ask for help. I hate being an invalid."

As she poured coffee into another mug for

him, she chewed her lower lip. What could she say? He'd always been so strong, so self-reliant, but all of that changed in a heartbeat—at least for now if the doctors were to be believed. With a cheerful smile plastered on her face, she handed him the coffee and poured another for herself.

"I'm sorry. I forgot to put them down last night. But Alex, this is just temporary, right? You'll be walking soon, and this will be a bad memory like a childhood nightmare you can push to the back of your mind. In the meantime, I'll rearrange the kitchen to make things easier, I should have done it already." His jade-green eyes met hers, and for a second she saw her old Alex, but it didn't last. As he took the cup, they hardened into blocks of marble, filled with the rage he'd barely held in check since they'd gotten home from Walter Reed.

No use arguing with him, she thought, as she bent and picked up the broken pieces while holding the towel in place. His eyes bored into her back. Remembering how he'd stared at her as intently last Christmas before he'd dragged her into the living room, and they'd made love for hours. If she let the towel drop would it distract him? Or just piss him off? He'd been in so much pain they hadn't been able to do much more than hug and kiss. Not that his kisses didn't light the fire they always had, but knowing if they went further how much pain he'd be in, stopped her from pushing it.

This Christmas wouldn't be filled with long walks on the beach at sunset, making love in every room in the house, and trying to make a baby. Nope. The tree was still in the attic, and there were no decorations to be found. She sometimes wondered if he even remembered that it was Christmastime. He was strung tighter than a guitar string, she didn't want to make it worse by reminding him of earlier years.

Pain and sadness etched lines on his face, he had deep grooves at the corners of his mouth that weren't there last Christmas. He did his best to hide his pain behind anger, but every muffled grunt squeezed her heart. He didn't want anyone's pity or sympathy—especially hers. How did she prove to him that his survival was the best gift ever, even if he never walked again?

Tossing the remains of the mug into the trash, she turned and flashed him, hoping he'd pull her into his lap and kiss her into oblivion.

Staring into his eyes, she had a moment of hope. His pupils dilated as his gaze slid over her curvy body, but that was it. He didn't reach for her. Didn't pull her into his lap. He just turned away.

As much as it hurt, she understood. She did. She knew him well enough to know he was proud and hated that he felt weak and helpless. That he couldn't take care of her. And that was the hard part for her. How was she going to get through that thick skull of his? "Give me a minute to get dressed, and I'll be back down to make us some breakfast."

"Don't worry about it. I'm not hungry, and I know you have a ton of work to do. I heard you tell Chloe you had deadlines this week, right? You might as well get to it."

"Yeah I do. But when did that ever stop us from having to eat? You have pills to take, and I need to have something other than coffee if I'm going to be creative."

"Since when did you start eating breakfast?"

He had her there. She'd never been one for morning food. Did she risk telling him that the doctor said she should eat better since she was trying to get pregnant? Especially now? But what the hell else could she say? "It's Chloe's fault or at least partly. When the girls are here, and I make them breakfast, Bella won't eat unless I eat too." It seemed like a good excuse as any and he appeared to be buying it, and he even laughed. Holy shit!

"That's classic. A kid is getting you to do what no one else could? Can I rent her for a while?"

"You know if you asked Logan he'd probably be happy to unload one of them for a bit. Chloe has her hands full." Their banter was like the old days and some of the sadness clouding her heart cleared like fog lifting, at least until his next comment.

"Yeah, well that wouldn't work. You already have a two-hundred-pound man to take care of, and work. I think you're over-allocated."

"I'm fine, besides you won't be like this forever. Anyway, I need to get dressed, I'm freezing."

After nodding, she watched as he wheeled over to the French doors to gaze outside at the backyard, then ran upstairs to do something about her now-dry hair to get out the knots and get dressed.

"Fuck." The longing on Lily's face kicked him in the gut. He wanted her with every fiber of his being, but not like this. Not with every movement stilted and pain-ridden. He wanted to lift her onto his lap and pleasure her until her eyes rolled back in her head and she collapsed against his chest. He wasn't sure he'd ever be able to do that again. Yeah, the docs said it was just a matter of time but it'd already been over seven months. How freakin' much longer? He loved her, but he wasn't good enough for her anymore. He couldn't give her what she needed or wanted. That was the problem. Every waking moment reminded him of what he was —helpless. He'd been taking care of himself since he was in high school and had started driving. Once he'd gotten his license, his parents decided he could take care of himself, and they'd left to travel the world for his father's business.

After that he'd seen them on the holidays—mostly—but it changed forever on September eleventh two thousand and one. They'd been in a meeting with their financial advisor at the World Trade Center when the planes hit. Away at college, he hadn't even known they were back in the states until he'd gotten the call from his father's secretary. It had been his sophomore year and after that, he and Logan, his best friend, joined the ROTC. The rest was history.

As he watched through the glass of the French doors, a pair of Sand Hill Cranes strutted along the edge of the lake. Their telltale squawk could be heard all around the neighborhood and sounded like someone was being killed. After a moment, a smaller version of the bird ran to catch up to the parents. Seeing the bird family reminded him again of what he couldn't give to his wife. They'd tried for years and now in a chair who would even give them the option to adopt? Sure, the docs said he'd walk again, but he knew from experience they said lots of things that didn't pan out. The coffee churned in the pit of his stomach as disappointment swirled in his mind.

He'd lied to Lily when he said he'd dropped the mug while reaching for it. If she thought about it, she'd probably have realized it too. He didn't want her to know the truth. Hearing the shower running upstairs, he'd taken the chance. Pushing up with his arms he made it to his feet as they'd showed him in PT. But that was as far as he got. He was upright for a whole two Goddamn seconds before the pain took his breath away. His fingertips had just reached the mug handle when he fell backward into the wheelchair, and the cup slid from his grip. He'd been fucking lucky to land in the chair and not on his ass on the floor. The mug? Not as lucky.

So much for getting better. Over seven damn months and he still couldn't take more than a step or two without pain so bad he'd almost passed out. What the fuck, man? Seriously. Did they think he was stupid? The more he thought about it, the angrier he grew. This is not the life Lily had bought into. Not to be stuck with half a man, to wait on like the child he hadn't been able to give her. And he didn't want her pity, she might try to mask it but he knew she had to feel it, her and everyone else he came across. Look at the poor soldier in the wheelchair, but don't look too close, you might have to talk to him.

Except Logan.

True or not, in Logan's face he saw guilt which was even worse than pity.

There was no way he'd wish this on anyone else and definitely not his best friend. Alex understood the guilt, and if he'd been in Logan's shoes he'd have felt the same way, but it didn't mean he'd accept it. Was it too much to ask to have his old life back?

Apparently.

Fuckin' A.

The roar of the C-120 overhead reminded him he wouldn't be going back to Afghanistan or on any other deployment. The doctors had been clear on that at least. There'd be no more front lines for him. It'd be a desk job—maybe. Or a medical discharge. Fuck that.

Before he'd realized it, he'd sent the mug sailing across the kitchen into the backdoor. His timing was perfect as usual. The door opened, and Logan had to duck as the mug flew by his face and shattered against the door frame. Logan shook his head as he shut it behind him, his shoes crunching on the shattered pieces of ceramic.

"Fuck, Alex. You trying to kill me?"

"Bad timing. Sorry." But he wasn't, sorry that is, well for almost hitting Logan, yes, but not for smashing the mug. For the few moments, the cup took to go from his hand to the door, he'd been in control. Crazy yeah, like by smashing it he had control, it was his decision, and he'd done it. Even if it was just an empty cup.

"Are you okay…" Lily's voice trailed off as walked into the kitchen and saw Logan. "Hey, Logan. Alex, what happened?"

"Besides this jackass trying to take me out? Yeah, everything's good."

"What?"

"It was an accident. I threw the mug at the door as he opened it. I didn't know he was there."

"Why would you…" Alex tried to keep his face impassive, but he was just itching for a fight. Lily, Logan, himself, anyone would do just fine. He was frustrated, he needed to do something, make a difference, not sit in a fucking chair and be waited on.

"Apparently, it's a bad day to be a mug in our kitchen," Alex answered while meeting her eyes, silently asking for her to drop it.

"Well damn. I guess I'll be going shopping, not that I ever need an excuse to spend money. Be careful, Logan. Let me get that cleaned up."

"I'll get it, Lily. I'm sure you have stuff to get done. Chloe said you were on a tight deadline."

"Are you sure? But yeah, I've got to get a presentation to the customer by five today. I still need to make us something to eat."

"Oh. I was hoping to take Alex out for a bit."

"Out? Fuck yeah. A change of scenery would be great. Wait, unless it's PT. I'll be happy to skip that shit." Lily shook her head, but at least she didn't look upset. He needed her to understand what he couldn't say to her, at least not yet.

"You have to take your pills…"

"You're not my mom, you're my wife. I'll be fine. Okay? Just get some work done. Logan won't let me starve. Right?"

"Yup, I'll make sure we get something while we're out. Deal?"

Lily sighed but nodded. "Sure. Will you be gone long?"

Alex rolled his eyes at his wife. The smothering needed to stop, or he'd lose it for sure. "I'll be with Logan. I'll have my phone, everything will be fine. You don't need to worry so much, okay? Seriously, babe."

He hadn't called her by any pet names for a while, and that seemed to get through to her in a way his other words hadn't. "I'm sorry…"

"Hey, Lily. You have nothing to be sorry for. Chloe is the same way with me. It's from always worrying about us. You can't stop cold turkey. But Alex is right. I won't let anything happen to him."

Nodding again, she stepped over and kissed Alex on the forehead. He fought the urge to pull her into his arms and kiss her the way she deserved. But he couldn't, not until he could be a real man again and he prayed that it would really happen.

After Lily had gone upstairs to her office, Logan grabbed the broom and swept up the remnants of Alex's mug. "What was that? Since when does your wife kiss you on the forehead and you just sit there?" Logan asked as he swept the pieces into a pile.

"I'm worthless. Stuck in this fucking chair, and she has to do everything. I hate it."

"Then do something about it. You're not confined to barracks. This isn't punishment. I've never known you to give up. Use those balls you're so proud of or do you need to grow a new set?"

"Fuck you. My balls are just fine. It's the rest of me that is fucked."

"Then what the fuck? Have you talked to her about stuff? Chloe would kill me if I tried that shit."

"No. I don't know what to say. I can't make

love to my wife, I can't work, I can't do the one job I love. What kind of a husband am I now? She needs someone who can be a real partner."

"That's bullshit, and you know it. She loves you. You need to get over yourself."

"Stop telling me what to do. I'm not a child."

"Damn it, Alex. You're my friend, hell, the brother I never had. But I'm not going to let you throw away your marriage out of some false sense of pride."

"I didn't ask your opinion. If you don't want to be here, no one's making you stay."

"You'd like that. It'd be easier, wouldn't it? Well, fuck you. Go get ready."

At first, Alex was going to object, but the pull of getting out of the house for something other than rehab was too great. It'd only been a week but home already felt like a prison.

CHAPTER 2

As Logan's car backed out of the driveway, Lily breathed a sigh of relief and sent up a small prayer. She'd hoped Alex's attitude would improve once they'd gotten home, but instead it had gotten worse. The sessions at Walter Reed had warned her that this could happen, but she'd thought she knew him better. He was a different person these days. Pain had a habit of changing people. If she hadn't known it before, she sure as hell knew it now and it didn't make it any easier to accept. His attitude went back and forth between being pissed off at the world and apologetic for needing so much help from her. It was maddening, and she wasn't sure who would lose it first, her or him.

The mugs could be replaced. But she refused to let him throw their marriage away, even if it's what he seemed hell bent on doing. Everything she'd tried so far to get through to him had failed, and she was running out of ideas. Maybe a frying pan to the head? Nah, that would be assault with a deadly cooking implement. She didn't think she'd do well in jail. There had to be some way to get through to him.

Grinning for the first time in a week, she booted her computer and got to work. The Walcott presentation needed to be finished by the end of the day to email it over for their review before she gave the presentation at Walcott's offices in the morning. In the BAI world—before Alex's injury—she'd have been done early. Instead, she'd barely started.

He was still drawing pay, but Lily wasn't sure what the future was going to hold. They needed her business to make sure they stayed above water. Besides, it kept her from having a meltdown. Work gave her something to focus on and was probably the only thing keeping her sane. Unfortunately, everything she'd tried to create since they'd been home had been total crap. It wasn't going to cut it. A job was a job, and she never went back on her commitments. Deadlines were made to be met, and she'd be damned if this time would be any different.

The Walcott Corporation was a new client. Her accountant had referred him while she was still up in Maryland, and she'd been happy for the work even though so far it had been a struggle. They bought the property the old Ramada Hotel had occupied until Hurricane Frank had destroyed it five years ago. Since then the land had been vacant. There'd been lots of speculation especially since it was prime beachfront property. Then last year it had sold. She had never heard of the Walcott Corporation, and she still didn't know much other than they were a privately-held company. As long as they paid their bills, she didn't really care. Although it did seem kind of odd that they'd come out of nowhere. There'd been a lot of speculation about what the property would be used for, and until they'd begun construction, no one had a clue.

Terrence Walcott along with five of his top staff had given her a tour of the facilities the day after they'd gotten home. The fitness complex included a state-of-the-art fitness center, spa, upscale restaurant, and shops more luxurious than anything else in Willow Haven.

It was a huge project, and a coup for Lily to have gotten the job, especially having been off the radar in town so long. But she wasn't going to look a gift horse, or in this case project, in the mouth. She had a good group of clients, but this could open lots of new opportunities if she didn't screw it up.

And screwing it up was all she'd done this week. It was like hitting her head against a brick wall trying to come up with something, anything, that she could present. Now she was out of time. Finally, though she'd had a breakthrough last night after Alex had gone to bed. After messing with it for four days, she'd come up with the perfect logo, and from there the rest had fallen into place. But that's how it always worked for her. If she could get one part, the rest was cake. Now she just had to hope that Walcott and his team liked it too.

Lily's stomach growled. Holy shit. It'd been four hours since Logan and Alex had left and she'd been working. Blowing her bangs off her forehead with an exhale, she flexed her neck and shoulders to work out some of the kinks that being hunched over a keyboard created. Then she stood up and stretched, relief that it was done lightening her mood.

She'd done it, put together the presentation and even better—she liked it—really, really liked it. The low rumble in her tummy was getting a bit louder and insistent. Then she remembered with all the distractions she had never eaten breakfast, no wonder she was so hungry. It sucked when your body got used to eating. She'd liked it better when she could eat once a day and be done with it. Once a day and a bottomless cup of coffee, at least when she was working on a project.

Giving into her body's demand for food, she figured she'd grab something then go over the entire presentation one more time before emailing it to Mr. Walcott's assistant, Enid Mercier. It never hurt to double check, there was nothing worse than sending an email or a report and finding a typo after you hit the send button. It was the stuff of her nightmares…or had been until Alex's injury. Now her dreams were filled with visions of her husband being blown to bits. The dreams had been coming with less frequency at least, but she longed for the time when she could have a full night of sleep without waking up in a cold sweat convinced her husband was dead.

As her foot hit the last step, she heard the kitchen door open. Perfect timing. Maybe they could have lunch together unless Logan had stuffed him full of crap earlier. That was a definite possibility, the two of them together were dangerous—not in a bad way—just always getting into trouble. She and Chloe had often joked that they'd never grow up and always act like twelve-year-old boys. Rounding the corner and entering the kitchen she called out.

"Hey. Did you have a good time, butthead?" Damn. She hadn't meant to call him that. It'd been one of the names she used to call him and she cringed inside waiting for his reaction. That's when she noticed he wasn't alone, Logan was there too, and he had a four-legged furry thing on a leash sitting next to him in the kitchen. A dog?

"Bringing home strays, Logan?"

"Nope, he lives here. Unless you're tossing him out? Oh wait, you meant the dog, didn't you?"

"Uh, yeah."

"He's mine," Alex cut in. It was the last thing Lily expected, and she'd hoped that Logan had gotten it for the girls. Except Chloe would have killed him.

"This is Hunter. He's a service dog. Logan put in a request after he knew when I'd be released from the hospital. He's trained and everything." The dog sat next to Alex like he was waiting for her approval. Lily had no clue what type it was. Brown and tan medium-length fur made him look like he was covered in scruffy patches. Not exactly the cutest pup ever. Then she looked into his chocolate-brown eyes. It was like he understood everything, Alex's pain and frustration, and her fear. How she could tell that she had no idea, she sure as hell wasn't a dog whisperer. But somehow, he seemed to see into her soul.

Maybe this would be a good thing. Alex smiled down at the dog. Smiling, really smiling—even the corners of his eyes crinkled up. That alone was a minor miracle. "Gee, Logan. Thanks." No sense in letting him off the hook that easily.

"You're welcome," Logan answered with a sheepish grin. He knew her well enough to expect an ass kicking. But anything that could make Alex smile like the old days was okay with her.

Lily moved closer to Hunter and crouched down until she was eye level with their new furry family member. "Are there any rules? Can I pet him?"

"No, he's mine." Alex's words and tone were so gruff, if she hadn't looked up, she'd have believed him. The smile plastered on his face took the sting out of his words. She'd been waiting for more than seven months to see that smile, and there it was. Thanks to Hunter. She was in love with him already. "Just kidding. You can as long as he's not working."

"Oh yeah. I almost forgot. Every day for the next two weeks, Alex and Hunter need to go for training at Paws for Hope. Will you be able to take him if I can't?" Logan asked.

"No problem." Lily held out her hand and let Hunter sniff her before she scratched behind his floppy ears. "What kind of a dog is he?"

"A mutt. Actually, a shelter rescue. The Paws for Hope people search shelters for dogs to rescue and train to be service dogs. Isn't that great?"

Lily nodded. It was amazing. Whoever

thought of it should be given a medal. "Logan, what made you think of doing this?"

"I can't take the credit. You remember Tag, right? I think you met him a few times."

"Yeah. He and Mac were injured a while back, right?"

"Yup. Just over a year ago. His Humvee hit an IED and Mac pulled him and a bunch of guys to safety."

"Yeah. I remember. We brought food over to Charlie and Shannon's house after we heard the news."

Logan nodded. All the men knew that the wives helped each other when one of their own was injured or worse. She shuddered at the memory. It had been a devastating week. Three dead, and four wounded in two separate incidents. But Logan's voice pulled her back to the present.

"It was his idea. He says Jackson, his dog, changed his life. I figured it couldn't hurt to see if I could get one for Alex. But of course, that was before I knew what an asshole he'd turned into."

"I'm right here, dickwad."

"I know, that's the beauty of it. I'm not talking about you behind your back." The look on Alex's face made Lily giggle, and damn if it didn't feel good. When was the last time she'd laughed? She couldn't remember. Hunter was in their house for less than ten minutes, and already she could feel the difference. Still as great as it seemed, she wasn't going to fool herself into thinking everything was fixed. But hopefully, it was the beginning.

"Okay. I'm out of here. Chloe's mom is coming over so we can go Christmas shopping for the kids. This is the first time I've been home to go with her."

"Better you than me. I hate shopping, and Christmas shopping is the worst. Being able to do it online has been my salvation."

"If I didn't know better, I'd swear you were an introvert, Lily."

"I've been called worse things." Standing up after giving Hunter one more scratch behind the ears, she hugged Logan and whispered, "Thank you. I don't know if this is permanent, but the change is amazing."

He didn't respond, just gave her a squeeze then headed to the door. "Talk to you later, asshole. Be good, or Hunter might bite your face off."

"Fuck you, Logan. And thanks, man."

"See ya."

"Do I need to go get some food and other stuff for him?"

"Yeah, food, dishes, and a bed too."

"Gotcha. How about some lunch and then I'll run out? I'm starving. You've got to be hungry too by now."

"We grabbed some Egg McMuffins on the way. I shouldn't be hungry, but I am."

"Is grilled cheese okay?"

"Yeah, sounds good."

While Lily got out the bread, cheese, and butter to whip up a couple of sandwiches, Alex told her about his morning.

"They gave us a tour of the facility, and we got to see some of the other dogs and how the training works. Then there was a ton of paperwork."

"So, he's yours? It's a done deal?"

"Is it a problem?" Alex's eyes were wary as they met hers. Damn, she hadn't meant anything by it. Just wanted to know if there was anything else that needed to be taken care of. Apparently, she wasn't done walking on eggshells yet.

"No, not at all. I only wondered if we needed to do anything still. Vet visit? Licenses?

More paperwork. That's all."

"Nope, it's all taken care of." As if to agree, Hunter woofed and wagged his tail. His tongue hung out of the side of his mouth, and she'd swear he was smiling. She'd never had a dog. Technically, she didn't have one now either. Hunter would be Alex's companion, but if he could bring her husband back to her, she'd be eternally grateful.

Alex wanted to kick himself for jumping down her throat over the simple question. He should have known she wouldn't have an issue with Hunter or anything else he wanted. Tension tightened his shoulders. A quiet whimper pulled his eyes away from his wife's back, and he looked down to meet Hunter's. The dog had picked up on his stress, just like the people at Paws for Hope told him would happen. He hadn't expected it to happen right away, though. A week or two, or after they'd completed their training, but within a few hours was remarkable. It's like Hunter understood him when no one else did.

The fur was soft under his hand as he slid his fingers over Hunter's head and scratched under his floppy ears. He was perfect. Not a pretty boy, but there was something about him that demanded love. Their connection had been instantaneous. Once their eyes met, it was like something in his heart unclenched. He didn't understand it, and he wasn't going to try. At least not yet. He needed the unconditional love Hunter could give him, and he would do all he could to make sure Hunter had all the love he could handle. He'd have his six—always.

"This is home now, boy. After we eat, I'll give you the grand tour. It won't take too long, we're relegated to the first floor for now." Hunter dropped his head onto Alex's knees. Considering he was in a new environment, Alex was impressed he was so relaxed. Paws for Hope knew what they were doing.

"Lunch is served. Sweet tea?" Lily asked as she turned holding the plates with their sandwiches. For the first time, he noticed the dark circles under her eyes, and the lines around the edges. His gut twisted. He'd put them there, of that he had no doubt. She hadn't signed on for this, having to take care of him twenty-four seven. It was unfair, and he hated it. Even though he loved her more than anything, he hated being around her. She was a constant reminder of how much their lives had changed. He didn't know how else to explain it.

"Tea's fine." It came out gruffer than he'd planned, and she winced. Maybe if he hurt her enough, she'd leave. Then he wouldn't have to feel guilty for putting her through this. Hunter nudged his hand, and he looked into the dark brown depths that seemed to understand everything. "C'mon, boy."

Alex wheeled himself to the table. Lily had moved one of the chairs into the dining room when they'd gotten back home so there'd be room for his wheelchair. It was another reminder of how different things were now. "Thanks."

"You're welcome."

Shitty way to treat his wife. He knew it, and the guilt morphed into anger. The anger and frustration bubbled just below the surface since he'd been wounded. Fuck. He wondered if it would have been better if he'd been killed, then he wouldn't have to deal with all of this. With any luck, Hunter would help him get a grip on it, but he wasn't sure how much a dog could truly help him.

Pain sliced along his spine, and he hissed out a breath. Fuck. The pills were wearing off, and the extra activity hadn't helped.

"Shit, I'm sorry. I forgot your pills." Before he could stop her, she'd gotten up from the table and grabbed four pill bottles off the counter and put them on the table in front of him. Thank God, she'd stopped short of giving him the individual pills. He could get his own meds.

"You didn't have to get them."

"I know, but it was easier for me."

"I keep telling you I can do it myself."

"Jesus Christ, Alex. What the fuck? You're my husband, you're hurting. You need to get over yourself. For better or for worse, remember?"

"Yeah, I remember. But we didn't count on this."

"Count on what? A temporary setback. It's not like you've lost your legs like Tag did. Yes, you're hurting, but you need to stop pushing everyone away. We're trying to help you, to make things easier. Is that so hard to take?"

"Fuck yes. Don't you get it? I don't want to *need* anyone's help."

Their eyes met, and hers were filled with

unshed tears. A muscle in her jaw twitched. He hoped she'd finish what she'd started, get it all out, everything she'd been holding back. She was right, too. Since they'd been home, he'd been trying to push her away. She was his wife not his nurse. He didn't want this for either of them.

"This sucks donkey balls. I get it. No, I don't know what it is like to go through what you are. But I do know that if the tables were turned you'd be all over me, doing everything you could to make sure I was okay and didn't need anything. Am I wrong?"

God dammit, she had him there. "No, you're not. But it's different."

"Don't do it, and you sure as hell better not say it. I know where you're going with this. I don't give a fuck if I have to take care of you, help you when you need it, or I'm the one who makes the money, so our bills are paid. Since when do you? We're a couple. I knew the risks from the beginning, you've been on how many deployments? And if you think about it, you're fucking lucky it isn't worse."

"You don't know what you're saying. I can't work anymore, at least not doing the only thing I ever wanted."

"True. But I'm sure you'll find something else that will be just as fulfilling. Logan gave it up. Mac gave it up, and Tag. Hell, you're not the first one to be wounded in action and dammit, you're alive. Don't you see how precious that is?"

Tears filled her eyes, and Hunter whimpered from their raised voices. Her argument took the fight right out of him. She was right. He was an ass. This was the woman he loved more than life. But it was also the reason he thought she'd be better off without him.

"I do know it. I'm not trying to hurt you, babe. I love you. But you have to see that you'd be better off without me. Be free to find someone who can be all you need in a man."

"Damn you, Alex. You are one stubborn SOB. Did you even hear anything I said?"

"Yes. I did. But…" Hunter licked his hand and then rubbed against it, successfully ending their argument.

His gaze went from his furry peacekeeper to Lily as she watched their interaction. A tear slowly rolled unchecked down her cheek. The part of the sandwich he'd managed to eat felt like a led balloon in his belly. If only he could turn back time and not been anywhere near the truck when it exploded. Instead, he couldn't even bring himself to wheel over to her and pull her into his arms for comfort. He didn't have it in him, not yet, maybe not ever again.

"How about we agree to disagree?"

"I don't…"

"Just think about it, okay? I'm going to go get what we need for Hunter. Is there anything else you want while I'm out?"

"No." The word hung in the air between them. She looked so sad, he had to do something. So much for his resolve. "Maybe you should pick up a few more mugs, our supply is kind of depleted."

The grin that spread across her face almost erased the dark circles under her eyes. Almost. He wanted her to be happy, hell, needed her to be happy. She was his everything. But he also knew it wouldn't be long before his frustration would eat at him until he lashed out at her because wasn't that how it went. You always hurt the ones you love the most, right? She never complained, and that made it all worse. At least for him. He didn't want to lose her but if that was the only way for her to get the life she deserved then so be it.

But it wasn't time to throw in the towel yet.

It'd only been a week, a long week, filled with anger and frustration for both of them. The word sorry wouldn't begin to cover the pain he'd put her through. But they had Hunter now, and maybe he was the miracle they needed.

CHAPTER 3

Slamming the car door as hard as she could didn't make her feel any better. God damn stubborn son of a bitch asshat doofus pigheaded jerk. Did he really think she didn't know what he was up to? She wasn't stupid. Thank God, she could see through him. Or she'd have really been devastated right now.

At least Hunter seemed to be making a bit of a difference. When he interrupted their arguing, Alex had looked at the dog, and his entire demeanor had changed. She didn't know how it had happened or why, but somehow her husband had fallen head over heels in love with a walking hair ball with chocolate eyes, and she couldn't be happier. If he could accomplish this after only a few hours, who knows how much he'd help Alex over all. Things were going to be better. The doofus would stop trying to push her out the door and remember their vows. She refused to accept anything else.

Where did one go for pet supplies? It wasn't something she'd thought about before. She knew they had some things in Publix, where she usually shopped. But she didn't have the first idea what Hunter needed. If she hadn't been so pissed, she would have asked Alex for the paperwork. No way was she going back in to talk to him now. He'd tried the little peace offering about the mugs, and it was good, but it was just a small gesture to assuage his guilt. And it wasn't enough.

None of this was his fault, and she didn't blame him even a little. She'd fallen in love with a soldier and knew the risks whether he wanted to believe her or not. Besides, he blamed himself enough for both of them. Grrr. Pulling her phone out of her purse, she Googled pet supplies in Willow Haven. Who knew they had three different chains in a five-mile area? She sure as hell hadn't, but she did now, and apparently, she'd driven by one on a weekly basis. Maybe she was getting old and forgetful. Nah, not at thirty-four. And she'd been away for over seven months, that was as good an excuse as any for not remembering.

She almost dialed Chloe to bitch about Alex for the fifty-millionth time, until she remembered she was shopping with Logan. Lily was happy for her. Chloe had practically raised the girls on her own, but now her husband was there to help for the first time. She tried not to think about the fact that if it hadn't been for Alex being wounded Logan would still be in Afghanistan. Alex hadn't told her, but she knew he'd been planning on volunteering for another deployment. It was part of his career plan, and as much as she'd wanted him home so they could have a family, she'd never have stood in his way.

How the hell had she missed the store? It was huge, at least as big at the Publix she shopped in. She really did have tunnel vision or something. After parking the car and going through the wide-glass doors, she stopped short. Not knowing where to begin, she must have looked as lost as she felt because it wasn't long before an employee approached her.

"Can I help you find something?"

"Yes. Everything."

"Uhh, okay. What kind of pet do you have?"

"A big fluffy mutt."

The skinny, pimply-faced teenager laughed. "Okay, c'mon I'll get you all set up, ma'am."

Ma'am? Did he just freakin' call her ma'am? WTF? Maybe it was time to rethink her skin care regimen? Who was she kidding, she couldn't be bothered. Or hadn't been before but Alex hadn't around twenty-four seven either. Maybe she needed to put a little more effort into her appearance. Snorting as she looked at her t-shirt and yoga pants, she couldn't hold back the whispered, "no shit!"

"Did you say something?"

"Nope, just thank you for your help."

"No problem, ma'am."

Rolling her eyes at the back of his head, she followed him to the food aisle, and her jaw dropped at the number of choices. It was a dog. It needed food. Seriously. "How do you decide what to buy?" she asked in awe, knowing she sounded clueless but didn't care.

"Well it depends on lots of things, whether you want to feed it all natural, how old the dog is, if it's overweight or not. But yeah, there are lots of options."

Nodding, Lily read the back of one of the bags. That was another thing, dry food or wet? She really hoped it would be dry. The wet stuff stank to high heaven. It was one memory from growing up she hadn't forgotten.

"We picked up Hunter today. I don't know much, unfortunately, except he's male, was rescued from a shelter, is a mutt. He was trained by Paws for Hope for my husband."

"Ahh, you should have said so. They're a great organization, I volunteer for them after school when I can." He selected a thirty-pound bag of food, then added a box of treats, and some green things he said would be good for Hunter's teeth.

"Great. Now I need some toys and a bed." Following him, with the full cart which was a lot heavier, they went up and down a few more aisles until she had everything on her mental list. "Is there anything else you think we might need?"

"You said he had long hair, right?"

"Yup. Well kinda. I guess it's more like medium tangled fuzz."

"Gotcha." He grabbed a brush and threw that in the cart. "That should do it. But if you need anything else we're open until nine every night but Sunday."

"Great to know." As she wondered how long the big bag of food would last.

After checking out and having a minor heart attack at the total, the kid helped her load everything into her car. Digging in her wallet she came up with a couple of bucks, but he wouldn't take it when she tried to tip him. Instead, he just thanked her for her husband's service. For a moment, she was dumbfounded as to how he knew, then she remembered she'd told him about Paws for Hope. That would do it. His nametag said Fred, and now all she had to do was remember it so when she came back, she could tell the store manager how great he'd been. It was a perfect plan, as long as she could remember his name. She was terrible with names. Maybe if she made a note of it on her phone. Oh yeah, that would work, then she'd forget she did that.

In a happier mood than she'd been in months, Lily stopped by Home Depot and picked up a pine wreath for their front door. Maybe it would push her to do more decorating or at least get the tree up. Damn. She hadn't even shopped for anyone yet. Her usual online buying spree on Cyber Monday hadn't taken place because she'd been in Maryland at the

Fisher House. Did she even have time to order and have it arrive before Christmas? Ugh. The last thing she wanted to do was go to the mall. It would be torture. Even worse than a zombie apocalypse.

The house was in one piece, at least from the outside. A good sign Alex hadn't started any fires while she was out. As soon as she stepped onto the driveway, she heard a dog barking. What the... Hunter! Duh. She didn't even think about barking, but it would make sense that the dog would warn Alex of anyone on the property. Grabbing the smaller bag of pet supplies and the wreath, she opened the front door where her men were waiting for her.

"Hunter let me know you were back."

"I heard," Lily said with a giggle in her voice. They sure didn't need a house alarm now. "How'd it go?"

"Fine. You missed Logan and Chloe though. They stopped by so she could meet Hunter."

"Too bad I missed her."

"She said she'd call you later."

"Great." Laying the wreath on the hallway table, she dropped the bag on the wood floor. "Be right back. I couldn't carry everything in one trip."

"Do you need help?" Why not? He could put the food on his lap and roll back into the house. It sure as hell made more sense than her hefting the thirty-pound bag.

"Yeah, c'mon." Hunter stayed at the side of the wheelchair as Alex followed her out to the car. Popping the trunk, she lifted the bag and put it across the arms of Alex's chair.

"Holy crap. This is all for him?"

"I said the same thing. Apparently, our little buddy is going to eat one every month or so."

"Seriously?"

"That's what Fred at the pet store said."

"Fred?"

"He was the one who helped me. I had no clue there were so many options. I mean they're dogs. Not that the cat area was any smaller. It was like a supermarket for pets. Oh, and he knew about Paws for Hope. He volunteers there after school."

"Small world, huh?"

"Yeah." Alex and Hunter followed her into the kitchen. After she washed Hunter's new bowls, she held one while Alex poured the kibble. She'd have to remember the bowls were in front of the Island now, so she didn't kick them and spill water everywhere. Who was she kidding, she'd do it at least three times by tomorrow. Good thing she wasn't betting with anyone.

What surprised her the most was that she and Alex were acting like the old days—almost. Teasing, talking and working together to get Hunter's area set up. Thank God, Logan had asked for a dog for him. She owed him big time.

※ ※ ※

It was great to hear Lily laughing. Twice in one day even. He didn't think he'd heard that since the last time they'd Skyped before the explosion, and it had been way too long.

As soon as they'd gotten the food area set up for Hunter, he'd looked to him for permission and then chowed down. The poor guy was probably starving. He didn't remember if they'd told him if he was on a regular schedule or not. He'd double check tomorrow when they went for their first training session, but for now leaving the bowl out all the time seemed like the best idea.

Lily disappeared and then came back in

holding the flowered wreath that had been on the front door. He'd seen the pine wreath and a pang of guilt made him wince. He'd completely forgotten it was Christmas time until he'd been out with Logan. The rehab center was decorated, but he'd managed to ignore it all. What to get for Lily was a big question? He'd asked Chloe when he'd seen her earlier, but she didn't have any idea. Normally she was his best bet, but this year everything was different.

"Nice wreath. When do you want to put up the tree?" Surprise showed on Lily's face at his question. She probably figured they were skipping it this year. He wasn't surprised. Last year his surprise had been getting leave for the holidays and two weeks alone with his woman had been the best gift.

The only thing that would have made it better would have been getting Lily pregnant. It's the only thing she really wanted, and he hadn't been able to give it to her then, and he sure as hell couldn't do it now. Looking back on things, it was a blessing that she hadn't gotten pregnant then. A baby and an invalid husband —she sure didn't need all that on top of working. His insides clenched tight.

Hunter nuzzled his hand and gazed at him

with soft chocolate eyes. Having someone so attuned to his feelings was going to be an adjustment.

"Uhh. I don't know. I wasn't sure I was going to this year."

"Why not? Don't you always put it up, even if I'm not home?" Her hesitation was the only answer he needed, but he still wondered why she didn't just come out and say it. He'd been an asshole, and he knew it.

"Usually."

"So, let's do it. Sorry, I won't be able to help you get anything down from the attic."

"No biggie. I usually do it myself, remember? Are you sure?"

"Yes, babe. I may be a dick and not the husband you deserve, but as you keep reminding me, we have a lot to be thankful for." The smile that spread across her face could have lit a dark room. He was glad he'd said something about the tree. It was such a simple thing, yet it made her so happy. He wished he could bring her to bed and rock her world, but she'd have to do all the work, and he wasn't having it. It made him feel like half a man.

"Before I do that, do I need to take Hunter out for a walk?"

"I can do it. He's my responsibility." He didn't mean for it to sound like it came out, so he forced a smile to soften the words. This helpless shit needed to end and soon or he'd have to find a way to set her free. "Did you finish your work? Maybe we should just wait until tonight?"

"I did finish, but I have to double check it and send it over. While you're walking Hunter, I'll take care of it. Then I'll get the decorations down. Okay?" Her excitement was contagious even though he tried to hold back. It would be too easy to roll over and let her take care of him. But he could do this for her. He owed her so much.

"Sounds like a plan." She dropped a kiss on his forehead, and once again he held himself back from responding. Instead, he watched her walk away, his eyes following the sway of her curvy hips and rounded butt. He almost drooled he wanted her so badly. In his mind, he pulled her onto his lap and kissed her until her toes curled. "Fuck me running." A woof from Hunter drew his gaze. "It's okay. I'm just frustrated. Can you grab your leash and we'll go for a walk?"

The dog did as he asked, and pulled the

leash from the table and trotted back to Alex's side. After giving him praise, he hooked it to his collar as they'd shown him at Paws for Hope, and then led Hunter to the French doors and outside into the backyard.

It didn't take long before he'd taken care of business and they were headed back into the kitchen. The wheelchair was barely through the doors when his cell phone rang. Fishing it out of his pocket he saw it was Tag or Bradley Taggart, as he was known by those who hadn't served with him.

"How's it going, Alex?"

"Good. A helluva lot better than this morning. I guess you heard about Hunter, huh?"

"Your dog? Yup. How are you two doing?"

"Me and the dog or me and Lily?"

"I was asking about the dog, but both matter." Tag was right of course. Both mattered in different ways, and both counted on him to get better. That was the question. Was it even possible? He'd been working hard, and so far, nothing much had changed.

"Hunter is great. I can't believe how in sync he is with me after only a couple of hours. How is that even possible?"

"You only see the tip of the iceberg, bro.

Once you've trained together, he'll be like an extension of you. He'll know when you're in pain, distress, or just if there is something not right. It's amazing how empathetic they are."

"Logan said you had one too?"

"Yup. Jackson, he's my life saver, literally. If it weren't for him, I wouldn't be here today. But that story is for another day."

"So, what's up? I'm guessing you had a reason for calling?"

"I wanted to make sure you were doing okay, and if you needed anything to let me know. I know you have Lily, Logan, and Chloe, but you're not alone. You have your brothers. Don't forget that."

"Thanks. I guess I have been. I should have had Lily bring me by your office to see you after PT."

"Fuck that. You've only been home a week, just sayin'. Once you're more settled, it'll be better. But there is one other thing. My sister, Anna, and her boyfriend, Ethan, are throwing a big Christmas party. She wanted me to invite you and Lily. And yeah I invited Logan and Chloe too."

A Christmas Party? Was he ready to be around other people yet? But then how could he say no when Tag was on the other end of the phone, and he lost a leg and an arm. He really was an asshole. He still had a chance of walking again on both of his own legs.

"I'll talk to Lily. When is it?"

"Sunday night. I know, not a lot of notice but you don't have to bring anything. Just show up. I'll text you the address. We all really hope you'll come."

"Thanks, Tag. I'll let you know."

"Later." Shit. He didn't know how he could get out of this unless Lily had other commitments.

"Everything okay?" Alex looked up from the phone he'd been staring at and laughed. Not only was she wearing an elf hat with a bell hanging down, but she had a huge smudge of dirt on her face. She looked like an overworked elf escaping from Santa's workshop.

"Yeah. It's fine." It was one of those moments he'd never want to forget, and before he said anything else, he snapped a photo with his phone. "You have dirt on your cheek."

"I do? Shit. Why did you take a picture then?"

"Because you're cute. Besides, now I have ammunition against you. You're always taking pictures of me at the worst moments and then you show Chloe. And I never hear the end of it from Logan."

"Whatever." It was her go to phrase, but this time she said it with a smirk. The day started out shitty but had definitely improved since he'd gotten home with Hunter. It's like they'd needed the distraction to remind them of what they had. Or remind him, Lily had been trying all along. He'd been the one to push her away.

"Did you get your work done?"

"Yup. Sent out the email with the presentation to the Walcott Team and confirmed our appointment for ten a.m. Shit. What time do you and Hunter have to be at training tomorrow?"

"Around the same time, I think. You can drop us off early on the way. They're over by the hospital. It won't be that far out of the way, right?"

"Nope. We live in Willow Haven, remember? Nothing is out of the way. You ready to play elf assistant?"

"Sure. Right, Hunter?"

"Woof."

She pulled another hat out from behind her back with a big smile. Now he knew why she'd had her hands hidden behind her back. She slid it on his head and adjusted it until she was satisfied.

"Is it good yet?"

"Yup. Just one more thing." Before he realized, she'd sat down on his lap and put her arms on his shoulders. "I love you, even if you are the most stubborn, pigheaded idiot of a man." He was about to answer her when her lips fit themselves against his. Desire raced through his body as her taste filled his senses. It would be easy to be lost in the kiss, too easy. But he couldn't. He needed to stop.

He took her hands in his and removed them from his shoulders. She pulled back and rested her forehead against his for a moment. "Why? What are you afraid of? It's obvious you want me as much as I want you."

"We've been over this."

"But…" Placing his index finger over her lips stopped her from continuing. He might be able to avoid the words but not the pain in her eyes. It seemed that all he did was hurt this woman.

"I think I'm going to go lie down. I'm kind of beat. Go ahead and decorate without me if you want."

As she lifted off his lap, she didn't say a word. She didn't have to. He knew her well enough to know exactly what was going on in her mind.

"C'mon, Hunter. Let's take a nap." The dog followed him as he wheeled out of the room. Lily never said a word, but he felt her eyes on him as he left the room.

CHAPTER 4

The beep of her alarm startled her awake. Staring at the ceiling she prayed that today would be a good day. Yesterday hadn't been a total disaster but after she'd kissed Alex it had changed. He'd gotten ornery again. It was her fault, she shouldn't have pushed it, but he'd been like his old self, and she hadn't stopped to think about what she was doing.

After he had gone to bed, she put up the tree and decorated it. She should have done the rest of the house too, but she just wasn't in the mood and ended up dragging most of the boxes back to the attic. The tree was up, it was better than nothing.

Then she rearranged the kitchen, making sure to move everything Alex could need to within reach and wheelchair height. She'd even rearranged the refrigerator shelves. It should have been done the first day they'd gotten home, but she was more concerned about taking care of him than getting the house ready. She couldn't blame him for wanting to be self-sufficient, but she wished he didn't feel like he had to be. Damn alpha males and their need for control over every situation.

"Right. But that's why you fell in love with him, doofus." She was back to talking to herself, sometimes she even answered. When you lived alone as much as she did, you had to talk to someone. Since they'd been back, she'd hardly seen Chloe. Maybe she needed to change that too.

They used to have coffee almost every morning when she wasn't pregnant or breastfeeding. She had to be done with that by now, right? Baby Andy was about five months old, so maybe not. How long did people breastfeed? Damn. She had no idea. Great friend she was. Everything had changed, though. While Alex was at Walter Reed, Logan's deployment ended, and he took a training position on base. It was the first time they both had their husband's home. Although having Alex there wasn't exactly fun and games right now. Patience wasn't her strong suit and his stubbornness was wearing on her.

Tossing back the blanket, she dragged her body out of bed. Carrying the boxes up and down the attic stairs reminded her she wasn't in such great shape these days. Too much desk work, not enough exercise. Fuck it. She liked her curves and Alex had never complained.

After a quick shower, she went downstairs to check on Alex and grab some coffee. She'd need all the help she could get if she had to put on makeup and clothing for the meeting. No PJs and slippers today. It reminded her how happy she was that she worked from home and didn't have to get dressed every day.

Alex and Hunter beat her to the kitchen and already had the coffee ready. She was thankful she'd rearranged the kitchen. "Morning, babe. How'd you sleep?"

"Okay. I think I might have had a nightmare. Hunter woke me up in the middle of the night licking my face."

His dreams had been getting worse not better the longer he'd been home. She'd tried to get him to join a group or see someone but not Mr. Stubbornpants. No way would he do that, it would admit weakness. What surprised her is that she hadn't heard him yelling. Usually, it woke her up. Hunter must have woken him before it got too far along.

"Good boy. You helped Alex." The dog thumped his tail a few times but stayed next to Alex's wheelchair. She wasn't sure how much she should try to interact with him, especially while they were getting to know each other. Less was probably better at this point.

"Yeah, he's a good boy. But I'm not sure the dog bed was necessary. He made himself at home in bed with me."

"Oh really? I see how it is. Hunter, you better not get too used to sleeping next to my man." She was teasing, but the look on her husband's face told her that he didn't take it that way. "I'm only kidding."

"Sure. You know what they say."

"No, what do they say?"

"That most things said in jest are really serious."

"Well *they* can say all they want, but I wasn't."

"If you say so."

"I do. Now I need coffee. Thanks for making it."

"No problem." He'd rolled over to the table and watched as she poured her coffee. She'd planned on taking it upstairs as she got ready but she'd rather have it with Alex. "I forgot to tell you, but we've been invited to a Christmas Party."

"When did that happen?"

"Yesterday when I was talking to Tag. Seeing you in the elf hat was a total distraction. The party is on Sunday at his sister Anna's house."

"Do you want to go?" She really expected him to say no. It had been hell to get him out of the house since he'd been home. They didn't know Anna and her boyfriend well, but she'd seen her around with Tag. Ethan was a detective with the Willow Haven Police Department and had helped bust a huge burglary ring in the spring.

"Not really, but I don't see a way out of it without sounding like a dick."

"No! You being a dick? Never. No one would believe that in a million years."

"Yeah, right. I know I've been a bigger ass than usual. After talking to Tag, it only made me feel worse. He's got it all together, and he lost limbs."

She didn't say anything to Alex, but she knew how hard a time Tag had at the beginning. It was a huge adjustment, and with PTSD too, he was a wreck for a long time. She prayed Alex's road wouldn't be as hard, but she knew that it wasn't always the injuries you could see that caused the most damage.

"I'm sure he'd understand, but it might be kind of fun, and you'd have your buddy with you."

"Yeah, I guess. Logan and Chloe will be there too. A lot of the guys from the unit who are on leave."

"Why don't you see how you feel after your training session?"

"Uh huh. You know it's after nine, right? Don't you have to be at your meeting at ten?"

"Fuck. Yup." She grabbed her mug and ran up the stairs. "Get ready, as soon as I'm dressed we're out of here."

"Yes, ma'am." She heard him even though she was halfway up the stairs. Again with the ma'am. Ugh. At least they had gotten through a cup of coffee without an argument. Little steps, Lily. Concentrate on the little things.

After running the flatiron through her hair, she applied some blush and mascara and giggled as she read the label on the tube. "I don't always wear mascara, but when I do it's 'Better than sex.'" It should be a commercial. They wouldn't be able to keep it in stock. Dressing in a navy suit and cream colored blouse, she finished it off with navy pumps. She was as ready as she'd ever be. Checking herself in the mirror, she didn't look have bad. Professional even. Then she stopped by her office, she grabbed her tote already packed with her laptop and backup, along with several copies of the printed presentation. This wasn't her first rodeo. Even though she'd have preferred not to do it in person, it wasn't because she couldn't.

Carefully making her way down the stairs, so she didn't end up on her ass, she yelled for Alex. "You ready? C'mon...load 'em up and move 'em out, big boy." When she didn't get a response, a sliver of fear chilled her to her bones. What if he'd fallen and she hadn't heard him? Shit. Rushing in to his room she expected the worst, but instead, it was empty.

"Alex?"

"We're waiting for you. Didn't you tell us to get a move on?"

Following the sound of his voice to the open kitchen door, Hunter and Alex were waiting by the car. She just had to put up the wheelchair, hopefully without messing up her outfit. After a brief wrestling match, she won, and the chair was safely stashed in the trunk. Nine-twenty. As long as they didn't run into any traffic, she'd make it to the meeting on time.

The car ride had been quiet, each of them focused on their own thoughts. Hers would be worrying if she'd missed anything for the presentation. While his were rehashing his nightmare. Thankful she'd been semi-distracted by her meeting, she'd let it drop about his dream. Too bad he couldn't push it out of his head as easily. Instead of a few times a week, now they were every night, and each time more vivid. When he finally woke up, he couldn't even remember where he was.

They got to Paws for Hope early for his training, so after she dropped him off he didn't go in right away. The weather was nice, Florida in December, low humidity and mid-seventies. Why not be outside while he could? Of course, his mind wandered back to last night's dream.

Hunter had helped, at least he hadn't fallen out of bed trying to run from the explosion. Every fucking time he closed his eyes the scene played out like a bad movie. The truck driving through the gate checkpoint and onto the base, the explosion minutes later. Seeing two of his unit tossed into the air as they ran from the blast. But he was never fast enough, could never get far enough away. Never save Bongo. That was the worst.

Seeing his friend lying in the dirt and sand, eyes open but unseeing, half his body missing. Even now so many months later, thinking about it made him break out in a cold sweat. As his heart tried to beat out of his chest, he thought he was going to pass out, when a hand pressed down on his shoulder. His first reaction was to reach for his M-4, the rifle he didn't carry anymore.

"Easy, Alex. You okay?"

Breathing in and out slowly, he calmed his heartrate and focused on the here and now. "You scared the shit out of me. Don't you know better than to come up behind someone."

"I was calling your name. Hunter knew I was there, he even nudged your hand. Didn't you feel it?"

Fuck.

No, he hadn't felt it or heard Cage call his name either.

"Sorry, bro. I didn't mean to make it worse."

"No problem. I was just lost in thought." The look Cage gave him said he wasn't buying it, but he'd let him get away with it for now. He didn't really know Noah "Cage" Jensen except by reputation. Ex-SEAL, highly decorated and retired. Logan said no one knew why he'd gotten out, or if they did, they weren't talking. Now he was one of the trainers at Paws for Hope.

"You ready to work? How about you, Hunter?"

Cage had been Hunter's original trainer, and he clearly loved him. Even though he didn't move from Alex's side, his tail thumped against the concrete. "Yup, we're ready."

As they headed to the training area located in an old converted warehouse, Cage asked him about their first day together.

"It was good. No problems, at least not that I know of. My wife picked up a bunch of stuff for him at the pet store. She's unsure of how much she can interact with him."

"When he's wearing his harness, he's working, and he shouldn't be distracted from his job. But if you're just hanging out, watching TV, sitting in the backyard, whatever, he can be treated like a regular family dog."

"Good to know. I should have asked yesterday."

"It's a lot to take in at first. But you can call anytime, it's what we're here for."

"I'm surprised at how in sync he is with me. I didn't expect that to happen for a while."

"Every dog is different. Hunter is extremely empathetic. We don't know his whole background, except for medical records, but he must have been well loved before he was dropped off at the shelter."

"I hope I can take care of him properly."

"You will. We'll show you how, but mostly he'll be taking care of you. Logan shared your background with us so we could find the right dog for you. He also said you'd been having a lot of nightmares since you came back."

"Fuck. Is nothing private?"

"We're not here to judge. The whole point of this program is to help you and the dog. Finding the right match is imperative and the more we know, the better. Since you were at Walter Reed, we couldn't meet you. Logan and

Tag filled in the blanks, it's not how we usually do things, but you had good references."

"Thanks. I think."

"You have good friends. Don't push them away. A strong support system can make all the difference with recovery."

"I guess. I don't want to need help."

"You were an Army Ranger, so it's not surprising at all. But if you want to move past all of this you'll need to."

"Who the hell asked you?" As soon as the words had left his mouth, he felt like a huge piece of shit. The shadow that crossed Cage's face told him more than he wanted to know and more than the ex-SEAL realized he was sharing. What the fuck was wrong with him? Why couldn't he keep a reign on his emotions? Why did he constantly want to rip everyone's heads off? He really wasn't fit to be around anyone, except maybe Hunter. For some reason, the dog helped to make him calmer, at least when it was just the two of them.

Maybe that was the answer.

"Let's get something straight. I'm not going to take any shit from you. I know you've been through some heavy shit, but a lot of soldiers have. You need to show people respect."

"You're right. I am sorry. I'll try harder." Cage nodded and continued into the warehouse.

The next two hours were spent putting Alex and Hunter through their paces. Teaching him how to communicate with Hunter when he couldn't use his voice. How to direct him to help, or get help for him.

When Lily returned to pick them up, he was more than ready to call it quits for the day. He wasn't sure if it was the lack of sleep, the training, or both, but he couldn't remember being this exhausted since Ranger training. He needed a nap.

CHAPTER 5

It was Lily's first visit to the beachfront offices of the Walcott Corporation. It was beautiful. The four-story glass building almost disappeared into the sky as it reflected the sky and water. It didn't hurt that it was surrounded by native plants and palm trees. As beautiful as it was, if you weren't looking for it, it was almost invisible.

After parking, she checked her lipstick in the rearview, then grabbed her case and took a deep breath. She was not a fan of big presentations and thought it would be just her and Terrence Walcott. But his secretary's email fixed that misconception, and let her know he'd invited the entire project team. The design she'd come up with was good, but that didn't mean the customer would like it, and the customer was always right. Mentally crossing her fingers, she walked through the automatic doors into the cool climate controlled building. What was the worst that could happen? If they hated it, she still had time to come up with something else.

Stopping at the reception desk, she signed in and was handed a visitor's badge. The perfectly made up receptionist told the meeting was in the fourth-floor conference room. The piped in classical music was at odds with the click of her heels on the marble floor as she walked across the lobby to the elevator. This was the most lavish building she'd been in since moving to Florida. It seemed like overkill for Willow Haven, but it wasn't her money.

The elevator doors opened, and an elegant middle-aged woman was waiting for her with a smile. "Ms. Barrett?"

"Yes. Lily Barrett."

"I'm Enid Mercier, Mr. Walcott's assistant. I'll show you where you can set up. They're all in a meeting but shouldn't be too much longer."

"Okay, great. Thank you." Lily followed the woman who looked like something out of her Cosmo magazine, from her Christian

Louboutin heels to the top of her perfectly-styled hair. Until that moment she'd felt good about her appearance, but now she was second guessing it. Her suit hadn't been cheap but not even close to Ms. Mercier's. What did they say? Dress for the job you want not the one you have. Well if they ended up tossing her out on her ass that was fine too. Yeah, this would be a coup for her little company, but she didn't need the work.

"Can I get you anything?"

"No, thank you."

"You can set up here, the windows will be dimmed, so you don't need to worry about the glare."

"Dim the windows?" That was a new one on her.

"Yes." She smiled and for the first time seemed more human than Stepford woman. "It's really quite ingenious." She pulled out her cell and clicked her screen a few times, and the windows darkened like a shade had been pulled over them, but you could still see outside. "It's fully adjustable all the way to opaque. Mr. Walcott incorporated every new technology available in this building."

"That is very cool. From what he showed

me at the fitness complex he's doing the same there."

"Oh yes. He believes that if you don't go all in, why bother?"

Lily hadn't picked that up when he'd given her the tour of the complex, but maybe she'd been too distracted about Alex. They'd only been back in Willow Haven one day when she had the meeting. Now it was six days later, but it already felt like months.

"From the looks of this building he's been very successful."

"Yes, you could say that." The man himself commented from behind her. Lily jumped. How the hell had he snuck up on her with all these marble floors. Did he hover above the ground too?

"Good morning, Mr. Walcott."

"Terrence, please. I'm looking forward to your presentation. I liked what I saw when I reviewed the mockups."

"Thank you. I'll be ready shortly. I just need to connect the laptop to a projector."

His assistant clicked another button, and a portion of the table top slid open, and a projector appeared out of the opening. She couldn't hide how impressed she was, and she caught Terrence grinning at her reaction.

"You'll see I don't do anything half-way, Lily."

"That's definitely obvious." A few moments later the rest of the team came in. As they took their seats around the large mahogany table, Terrence did the introductions as the ten-people focused on her with various degrees of interest. Talk about wanting to sink into the floor.

"Please welcome Lily Barrett of OLB Designs. I asked her to come up with an advertising campaign and do some mockups for the web presence."

"What? Wait a minute, I had it covered. Markman's created the entire campaign and started work on the site already."

"I had Enid contact them to cancel. I didn't fit my vision for the complex."

"But…"

"Harrison, we'll discuss this offline later." Harrison Chandler, Terrence's executive vice president, looked like he swallowed a frog but he kept his mouth shut. He could have been one of the preppy asshats she'd avoided in college, right down to his slicked back dirty-blond hair.

Men like him gave her the heebie-jeebies. It's not that he wasn't attractive, but it was in a used car salesman type of way. The thought relieved some of the pressure building in her shoulders.

After the initial objection from the douchenozzle, the presentation went well. At least that's the feeling she got. There were some good questions and after all the feedback she had some tweaks to make if she got the job. But she figured the look of admiration on Terrence's face was a good sign. There was something odd about the man, but she couldn't figure out what it was that bothered her about him. From the moment she met him she'd felt something was off like he was trying too hard or something. But that didn't make sense. It was obvious he was exactly what he presented to be, a man who knew what he wanted and made sure he got it.

A few of the project team approached her after the meeting while she was packing up. If their questions and comments were any indication she had the job in the bag. She hoped they'd give her the 'official' okay soon so she could get to work making her mockups come to life. She couldn't wait to tell Alex and Chloe about it. That made her wonder how his training was going. She checked her phone, but there were no texts from him, just one from Chloe wishing her good luck.

After thanking Enid for her help, she grabbed her bag and planned on leaving. She hadn't realized Terrence's office was on the same floor, she should have, though. It was the top floor, and it was only the best for Mr. Walcott. Chatting with Enid as she headed to the elevator, she almost collided with Harrison Chandler as he threw open Walcott's office door and stormed out.

"Well damn. What's the hurry?" She stopped herself before she used her nickname for him. That would have been a disaster. Instead of answering, he glared at her and continued down the hallway.

"Are you okay? He didn't bang into you, did he?"

"No. I'm fine. He just startled me."

"Can I get you anything, Mr. Walcott?"

"Please get Jameson on the phone. Let me know when you have him. Lily, do you have a moment before you go?"

"Yes, sir," Enid replied, and then smiled briefly at Lily.

"Did you have some questions?" Lily asked

as she followed him into his office. He closed the door behind her, and the hairs on the back of her neck shivered. It was so weird. There was no reason at all for her reaction to him, but she couldn't deny it.

"No questions. Just wanted to let you know you have the job. I'm impressed with your work, Howard was right to refer you to me. I'll have to send him a bottle of that forty-five-year-old scotch he enjoys." He said it like she knew that her accountant liked scotch let alone forty-five-year-old stuff. He did her taxes, that was the extent of their relationship. But she did owe him something for recommending her company.

"Excellent. I look forward to working with your team. Who will be the point of contact for the project?"

"I'd prefer you run everything through Enid and she'll see I get it. If I need to bring other members of the team in, I will." It seemed strange to her. He was the CEO, so why take such interest in one project? Especially when it was clear, he had a very capable team. There was something off about this whole thing. But was it weird enough for her not to take the job?

Nope. She'd pull her big girl panties up and deal with it.

"No problem. I'll have the next round of designs ready for you by next week unless you're closed for Christmas week?"

"Next week will be fine. Thank you, Lily." He reached for her hand. It was dry, thank God, but cold like marble and made goosebumps stand up on her skin. Thankfully her arms were covered by her suit jacket.

Anxious to get outside, she thanked him again and made her way to the elevator. After dropping her badge off at the reception desk, she stepped into the bright, warm sunshine. Her tension drained with each step further from the building. Glad it was over, she couldn't wait to get out of her 'dress-up' clothes and shoes. Her feet were killing her. She probably needed to wear heels more and slippers less. Nah. She couldn't give up her fuzzy slippers.

The sound reached her before she saw it. Arguing. One of the men was Chandler, but she had no idea who the other ones were. Definitely not happy campers. She wanted no part of it and hoped she'd be able to get out of there before they noticed her. Too bad she wasn't that lucky. She was so close to making it when there was a tap on the driver's side window. She hadn't seen him approach and her heart jumped in her chest.

Motioning for her to roll down her window, she debated whether to floor it and get the fuck out of there or to do it and see what he wanted. It was a parking lot in the middle of the day, so she gave in and rolled it down. It was safe, wasn't it?

"I don't know what you said to Walcott, but you better watch yourself, bitch. I can't have you fucking up my plans. You're going to turn down the job do you hear me? If you don't, you'll be stepping into some deep shit especially with that invalid husband of yours."

"What I understand is that you're out of your mind. You're not the boss or the boss of me. If you have a problem, take it up with Mr. Walcott. And my husband is an Army Ranger and can take care of himself, so I'd be careful who you're threatening." If he'd been a cartoon steam would have shot out of his ears. His face turned red, and he looked like he was vibrating with anger. One look at the rage showing in his cold hard eyes and she figured it was time to go.

The drive to pick up Alex and Hunter at Paws for Hope was spent rehashing the threats Chandler had made against Alex. It was surreal; like she'd walked onto the set of a Lifetime movie. Still, his threats seemed real enough, but she'd never been the type to back down. What could he really do? Debating whether to tell Alex she opted for not. He had more than enough going on right now without worrying about her. Especially when she was almost sure it was an empty threat. Almost.

Alex and Hunter were waiting with a giant when she pulled up. He wasn't really a giant, but with Alex in the chair, he sure looked like it. The guy had to be at least six foot five and ex or current military. Not someone whose wrong side you'd want to get on.

"Hi. I hope you weren't waiting long."

"Not really. Lily, this is Cage. He's helping me and Hunter learn the ropes."

"Nice to meet you." She smiled up at him, having to take a step backward to see his face, as she held out her hand. His closed around hers like she was a child. Definitely a giant of a man. "I hope we're not keeping you from anything?"

"Not at all. We only got out here a few

minutes ago. I'm enjoying the weather."

"You must be new to Florida then?"

"Yeah. I've only been here a few months. It's going to take some getting used to. But I can't say I'll miss shoveling snow and dealing with the ice."

"You'll get used to it pretty fast. Although there are some things that are better in the cold," Alex said as he rolled over to the car and stood long enough to rotate into the passenger seat. Hunter jumped into the back as soon as she opened the door. But Cage grabbed the chair before she had a chance to reach for it.

"Where do you want this, ma'am?"

"Ugh again with the ma'am. Do I look old to you?"

Cage's chuckle was deep and throaty. "No ma'am, just habit."

With a sigh, Lily opened the trunk. "If you say so. But that's twice in two days, and I'm feeling old quick." Once they were out of eye and earshot of Alex, Cage leaned close to her ear.

"How is he? I mean really?"

Startled, she wasn't sure how to answer his question. She didn't know him, but it didn't mean he wasn't a friend of Alex's. She didn't usually discuss their personal business with anyone—except Chloe and Logan. But they were more like family.

He must have sensed her hesitation. "It's okay. I saw how irritable he was yesterday and even though he was a bit better today, there is something going on with him. I can see it, and Hunter is picking up on it."

"Well, yeah I guess. He's not happy. Really, not happy. But I'm hoping once he gets rid of that chair things will be better."

Cage nodded and started to back away, then stopped and handed her a card. "That's my personal number. If either of you need anything, with Hunter or anything else, you can call that number anytime. Okay?"

"Yeah. Thanks. I'm sure we'll be fine." She smiled and took the card. He was more than a little intense, but his heart seemed to be in the right place.

"Well, you have it just in case." He walked around the side of the car and shook Alex's hand. "See you tomorrow. You be good."

"Hunter's been great," Alex said defensively.

"I meant you, bro." Cage laughed and waved as he walked away.

"What an ass."

"Really? Maybe you should see about getting a new trainer then?"

"Nah. He's not that much of an ass. I like him. He's had it hard."

"You know him?"

"Not really. I know *of* him, though. He's a SEAL or I guess ex-SEAL now."

"And he went from being a SEAL to a dog trainer?"

"Yeah. At least for now I guess. He's got a way with the animals."

Lily nodded. "How did the training go?"

"Great. Hunter's doing great, me not so much. I kept fucking up. Lucky for me Hunter won't hold it against me. Right, boy?"

The fluffy canine leaned over the back of Alex's seat and licked the side of his face.

"How did the presentation go? Did you get the job?"

"It went well. Everyone seemed to like it. Well almost everyone. But the main thing is that Walcott liked it, and apparently, that's all that matters there. Definitely not a democracy."

"What do you mean? I thought you said there was a team in charge of the fitness complex."

"I did, and there is, but I don't think anything gets done in that company without Walcott's fingers in the pie."

"Not a very efficient way to run a company, is it?"

"You wouldn't think so. But if his building is any indication, he's doing well, or at least the company is. I couldn't really get a feel for the whole thing. It was strange. He has an assistant who runs the office, but he has to have his hands in everything."

"You'd think he'd be all about delegation."

"Exactly. It's what would make the most sense. Anyway. It's his business. He did hire me to do the work. But if he's always like he was today, he's going to make me crazy with his micro-managing."

"Want me to have a word with him?"

"No! I mean, I can handle it. I've been working with people like him for a long time, remember? It's what I do while you're off saving the world."

"I know that. But I'm home now and can help. Besides, I need to do something." Her eyes were focused on the road, but her eyebrow arched in surprise. He hadn't shown much interest in anything at all. But Cage was right, he needed to get his head out of ass. There were thousands of other soldiers who'd come home injured, like Tag. Alex sighed. The military had been his life, and he'd loved it, but maybe it was time to see if there was something he could do to make him feel useful again. Be a man again, the man his wife needed.

"You are, you're doing PT almost every day and now training with Hunter too."

"That's not what I mean."

"The doctors said you weren't supposed to do much until they could get that other piece of shrapnel out."

"I know. But what if that never happens? What am I supposed to do? Sit on my ass and be waited on for the rest of my life?"

"No. Now you're just being ornery."

"I don't want to fight with you. I'm trying, I am."

"So am I. I know it's hard, baby, but you can't give up on you or us." He was still tempted to do exactly that. It would be so much easier. Thankfully, they pulled into the driveway before he could think about it much longer.

"I'm sorry it's so hard."

"Stop. It's not hard, it's love and marriage." Her eyes said she believed what she was saying. He just wished he could, and because of that, he didn't know how to answer her either. But she saved him from having to when she got out of the car to get his wheelchair. He leaned over the seat and opened the back door so Hunter could get out. He probably had to pee.

"Go on, boy. Just stay by the driveway." Hunter jumped down and did exactly that. After taking care of business, he came over and sat down and waited for Alex to get out of the car.

"I want to get out of these clothes, then I'll make some lunch. You have PT at three."

"Got it. Are you sure you can take me? What kind of deadline are you on for Walcott?"

"You know, that was the one thing he didn't say. I guess I'll have to call Enid and check."

"Enid?"

"Yeah, his perfect assistant."

"I can't remember the last time I heard of

someone named Enid. Is she really old?" He asked as he followed her into the house.

"Not sure really. She had gray hair, but that doesn't mean anything. I've been pulling them out of my hair."

"Ohh my ol' lady is getting to be an old lady."

"Funny. Just remember, you're six months older than me," she said and stuck her tongue out as she headed upstairs to change.

"C'mon Hunter, let's see if we can make lunch without waiting for Lily." Trotting alongside while Alex rummaged in the kitchen he found all the ingredients to whip up two amazing peanut butter and jelly sandwiches. Maybe not amazing to anyone else but when he thought about it, it was probably the first meal he'd ever made for his wife. Then he even managed to refill Hunter's food bowl without dumping the entire bag on the floor. It was going well until lifting the food sent pain shooting up his spine and took his breath away. This was what fucking sucked. The constant pain drove him crazy and when it spiked he couldn't breathe. It was time to talk to the doc and find out if this was his new normal or if he'd ever get better.

"You made lunch for me?" It was sad she was so shocked, but it reaffirmed his decision to try to do more for her. If he wasn't going to be able to be who he was, he had to find another way to show her he would always take care of her.

"Uh huh. Hunter helped a bit. Or at least, he tried." Alex smiled and hoped it made up for the almost fight they had in the car. Depression was not something he'd been familiar with, but it seemed that he was now, with the PTSD and just the overall anger and frustration about life had turned him into a mean ass bastard.

"Thank you. Seriously. Thank you, baby." Her hand grazed his cheek as her lips slid over his in a soft kiss. After yesterday's fiasco, she was probably afraid to push him, and he couldn't blame her.

"You're welcome—seriously." Hunter laid down at his feet after he got settled at the table. Ripping off a piece of the sandwich, he leaned over and offered it to his furry buddy. Without a hint of hesitation, he took it from Alex's hand like he'd been doing it his entire life. Alex wished there had been more information about Hunter's background, but Paws for Hope could only get what the shelter had—which was that he had been well taken care of and had all of his shots.

"How did the training session go? That Cage guy seemed pretty intense."

"You could say that," Alex said with a chuckle. "It's the SEAL in him. They're worse than us Rangers."

"Is that even possible?"

"Oh yeah, but no one is as bad as the Delta guys. But hell, if you're not military and sometimes even if you are, you can't tell who they are unless you're on a mission with them."

"I had no idea."

"Well, it's not something anyone talks about. Now I have to kill you." Lily giggled and pretended to be scared.

"What's the training like?"

"Repetition, practice understanding each other mostly, I guess. Or me understanding him. Like learning his cues when he's trying to tell me something. Then he learns about me too."

"Sounds cool. Maybe one of the sessions I can stay and watch."

"I'll check, but it might be too distracting."

"No problem. I get it." She looked a little

disappointed and Alex decided he'd check with Cage tomorrow.

"What kind of a deadline are you on for the Walcott job? Do you want me to see if I can get someone else to drive me to PT? Logan might be able to."

"It's okay. I can take you. It's only an hour. I'll give Enid a call after I finish this delicious sandwich you made. Hopefully, she'll know what the milestones are for the project and the final timeline. It is kind of weird he didn't mention it. You'd think it would have been one of the first things he'd tell me. But then again the vibes in the office were so weird."

"You said that earlier. Weird how?" A slight hesitation let him know that there was more going on than she was telling him, and he didn't like it one bit. But for now, there wasn't much he could do about it.

"I'm not sure how to explain it, just like some kind of undercurrent for everything. Like I saw one level of stuff, but there was all this other stuff going on that I couldn't see. I don't know." She shrugged and chewed slowly as if considering how to explain it to him. He read her expressions too well. He might have spent most of their marriage away, but he knew his wife. There was something worrying her about this job, or Walcott or both. If she wasn't going to tell him, he'd just have to do some digging on his own.

"You know, it was probably nothing. Just me overreacting. This is the biggest job I've gotten since I started OLB Designs. And I've only been doing small quick jobs while we were in Maryland."

"Makes sense to me." It did, but he wasn't buying it. If he couldn't get her to open up, it might be time to give Chase Brennan a call. He'd started a security firm after he left the SEALs. "Just remember I'm here now, and you can bounce shit off me anytime."

"Thanks. But it's nothing really. Anyway, you have enough to deal with, speaking of which you might want to rest before PT."

Shit. PT wiped him out on a good day, and he was already exhausted from the training with Hunter earlier. He needed to work harder, build up his stamina, he'd spent way too much time wallowing in pity and pain. It was time to get over himself.

Lily got up and took their empty plates and put them in the dishwasher. Then grabbed a bottle of water. "I'm going to see if I can get a

CHAPTER 6

Alone in her office, Lily pulled her laptop of out of her bag and plugged it in. She could have checked her mail from her phone and called Enid downstairs, but she hoped to get some information from her about vice president douchenozzle and his scary sidekicks.

"Terrence Walcott's Office. Enid Mercier."

"Hi, Enid. It's Lily Barrett."

"Ms. Barrett. How can I help you?"

"I checked my notes after I got back to the office and I didn't see any timeline for the products. Do you have a schedule you can send me?"

"I thought we discussed..." Her voice trailed off, and Lily heard the clicking of computer keys. "That's right, Mr. Chandler interrupted the meeting, didn't he? Yes, there is a schedule. I'll send you an email shortly."

"Great, I appreciate it. I know Mr. Walcott is in a hurry to get this started."

"Yes, he is, and he was very impressed with your presentation. This is kind of a pet project for him." It was the opening Lily had been hoping for.

"I was wondering if he was always so hands on? Especially with such a large project team in place." No answer at first, had her wondering if she'd overstepped some invisible line.

"Very observant of you, Ms. Barrett. He is involved in every aspect of his business, but as I said this is very important to him."

"I see. I didn't mean to sound like I was criticizing him. It's just Mr. Chandler was so adamant about his selection."

"Mr. Chandler is usually very professional. I was quite surprised to see him react that way. But Mr. Walcott is planning on going ahead with your plans, so you don't have to worry. I'll forward any information on work already completed."

"Thank you, again. If Mr. Walcott has any questions, just give me a call."

"We will. Goodbye, Ms. Barrett."

"Good bye."

Enid Mercier would be a tough nut to crack that's for sure. She'd hoped to get a bit more information out of her. But at least she didn't have to worry about the douche. It looked like he'd dug his own grave. The dull ache in her shoulders eased as she leaned back in her chair. She'd be fooling herself if she didn't admit that he'd scared the crap out of her, and she still didn't know how she held it together and got the hell out of there.

There wasn't much in the way of notes from the presentation. The weirdness of the meeting had been a distraction, from her usual frantic note-taking. Opening a new file, her fingers flew over the keys as she tapped out what she remembered and some new ideas she'd come up with.

The ringing of her cell phone broke her concentration a short while later. Checking the screen, she saw it was Chloe.

"Hey, brat. How the hell are you?"

"I'm good. Beat but good. You'd think I'd be used to having three kids by now."

"Yeah, except you have four, don't you?"

"Four? Oh shit, yeah Logan qualifies." They'd hardly seen each other since Alex was wounded. Chloe had been there for her until she'd flown to Germany to be with him for his second surgery, the first had been in the field hospital at Bagram Air Force Base. With baby Andy coming a few months later, she'd had her hands full too. Lily was glad Margie, her mom, had been able to help until Logan had come home.

"Yup. I really appreciate what he did for Alex though. Hunter is already making a difference."

"Thank God. I was worried about both of you."

"Me too. He's still a jerk about some things. But I haven't wanted to hit him with the frying pan today, so I guess that's progress."

Chloe giggled. "Yeah I'd say. How did the presentation go? It's a huge thing, I saw a write up in the paper today about Walcott and the whole project."

"Really? It went well, mostly."

"What happened?"

"Nothing. Okay, maybe a little something. The asshole VP flipped out when Mr. Walcott told me I had the job. Totally disrupted the meeting."

"What an asshat." Lily heard Chloe's

younger daughter, Bella, yell about the bad word. Those girls and their curse jar. One of these days she was going to smash that thing. "Sorry, Bella. I'll put money in later. Now go play with your sister. I'm back, sorry. So, what happened after that?"

"It sort of broke up the meeting. They went into Walcott's office. We could hear them yelling but not clearly enough to make out what was being said."

"Sounds like he's a real winner. But you got the job?"

"Yeah."

"Congrats. It's going to bring you a lot of visibility. This might be a turning point for you and your company."

"Yeah, it could be. As long as I don't fuck it up. Or someone else fucks it up for me."

"Who would do that? Alex?"

"No, the douchenozzle. When I got out to the parking lot, he was having a yelling match with some seriously scary looking dudes. Then he saw me and came over and told me to not take the job, and threatened me and Alex."

"Holy shit. Bella stop listening to my conversation and go play, or I'll find some chores for you. That girl is going to be the death of me. Anyway, did you tell Alex?"

"No way. I don't need him getting all riled up about this. He's on edge enough already. He had another bad nightmare last night too. I hate that he won't let me sleep with him, but at least he has Hunter. When I checked on him, Hunter was sleeping snuggled against him. I'd be jealous if the dog wasn't so damn cute."

"Well, I think you need to tell him. What if the guy is crazy and comes after you?"

"I doubt that. Enid Mercier, Walcott's assistant, says he's normally very professional."

"But what about the scary guys?"

"I don't know. But I'm not going to let some asshole tell me what I can or can't do."

"I don't like this. You should tell Alex. Do you want me to talk to Logan?"

"No. Definitely, no. I promise if anything else weird happens I'll talk to Alex, or maybe I'll call Ethan, Anna's boyfriend. He's with the Willow Haven PD, he might be able to give me an idea or two on how to handle him."

"Good idea. You'd better tell me if anything else happens."

"I will. Shit. I've got to go. Alex has PT."

"Okay, call me later. Oh, and we have to talk about the Christmas Party."

"I'll call you. But I've got to go, or we'll be late. And his therapist gets a real bug up his butt if we're late."

After hanging up with Chloe, Lily pulled on a pair of jeans and a t-shirt since she'd changed back into PJs when they'd gotten home earlier. Everyone thought she was weird, but her brain worked better when she was relaxed and comfy. She used to wear them out, at least to get coffee or when she was helping Chloe with the girls, but after so getting a shit ton of crap she'd started wearing "real" clothes whenever she went out. At thirty-four, she figured it was time to dress like a grown up, at least outside of the house. Most of the time anyway.

Shit. There was no way they'd get to the rehab center on time, especially if Alex was asleep as she expected. He'd look worn out from the training with Hunter. But he surprised her. Both he and Hunter were ready and waiting for her when she got downstairs.

"I was wondering if I was going to have to send Hunter to get you."

"Sorry, Chloe called, and I didn't realize the

time. We might be able to make it without being late or only a few minutes late."

"Only if you drive like a mad woman. Damn, what the hell am I thinking? Do you ever not drive like a mad woman?"

"Yup. When I have the kids in the car. They tattle to Chloe."

Alex laughed like she'd hoped. She really didn't drive like a mad woman. Okay, maybe sometimes she pushed the speed limit a bit, kind of, maybe. But she'd never gotten a ticket so she couldn't be that bad, right?

"Okay, c'mon sexy, let's get you and your master into the car."

"You're calling the dog sexy?"

"You have a problem with that?"

"It depends."

"On what?"

"On what you think I am, if you think that the dog is sexy."

"Well hmm. As soon as I figure it out, I'll let you know. Now hustle it up, I really don't want to get yelled at twice in one day." She held the door open while Alex wheeled out to the driveway with Hunter by his side. She'd slipped about the yelling, with any luck he hadn't heard what she said.

"When did you get yelled at?" Shit. So much for not noticing.

"It's not important." She hoped he'd drop it. And she went to put his chair in the trunk as he got himself buckled in. If she kept this up, she'd have some pretty impressive muscles.

"It happened at the meeting, right?" Lovely. Obviously, he wasn't going to drop it. Damnit. Stalling while she tried to come up with an answer, she put on her seatbelt and started the car, but she felt his eyes on her. He wouldn't be put off for long.

"It wasn't a big deal."

"No one should be yelling at you. Especially not people you're working with."

"Seriously? This is coming from you? Who yells all the time lately? And is in the Army and got yelled at for the first six weeks in boot camp?"

"I shouldn't be yelling at you either. I'm sorry for that." Wait, what? Did he just apologize for yelling? Sweet baby Jesus. Maybe she'd get her old Alex back after all.

"True. But I understand why you have been. You're in a lot of pain, and you're frustrated, and God only knows what kind of shit is going on in your head since you won't talk to me about it."

"It's a lame ass excuse. If any of my men were treating their wives this way, I'd give them hell. You deserve so much better."

"There is no deserve in this, Alex. Damn it. Why can't you get it through your thick skull? I almost lost you. When I got that phone call, my entire life stopped. It was like my world imploded. But we were given a gift. You survived. I don't care if you never walk again as long as we're together. You are my world, my sunshine, my best friend, and the other half of my heart." Shit. She tried but couldn't stop the tears from filling her eyes. Why couldn't he get it? It seemed so clear to her.

"I'm sorry."

"There's nothing to be sorry for. Just don't throw this away. I know what you've been thinking." He looked surprised when she glanced at him. But they'd been together too long for him to be able to hide anything from her. It's why she wanted to bean him with the frying pan. Stubborn ass.

"I guess I'm not hiding my feelings as well as I thought."

"I guess not." She was turning into the

parking lot of the Rehab Center when she noticed the brown car behind her. She couldn't make out the driver, but the car looked like the one from the Walcott parking lot. Were they following her? Why hadn't she looked around when they'd left the house? Stupid.

"You don't have to wait if you have stuff to do."

"It's okay. I'm not going to drive back home for forty minutes. Maybe I can find Tag and talk to him about the Christmas Party."

"Sounds like a plan." Checking the parking lot as she pulled Alex's wheelchair out of the trunk, she didn't see any sign of the car. It was probably just her imagination. The confrontation with douchenozzle must have gotten to her even more than she'd thought.

Alex was wheeling toward the sliding doors when he stopped and turned around. She waited and wondered what was up. He surprised her when he turned the chair around and stopped in front of her. Before she could say anything, he took her hand and pulled her down until she was eye level.

"Lily, I know I've been an ass lately."

Where was this coming from?

"I can't imagine my life without you, and

trust me, I've tried these last few months. I think you'd be better off without me, but I can't let you go. I'm really sorry for all I've put you through. I hope you can forgive me. I'll try harder. I promise." Damn. There she went again. Tears. What was wrong with her, she wasn't usually so mushy, but today she couldn't seem to stop.

"I love you, babe. There is nothing to forgive…" She had more to say, but the glass doors slid open behind them revealing the therapist from hell aka Carlos.

"Hey slacker, you planning on working today or blowing me off? You're not going to ever get out of that chair if you keep up this shit." Carlos was one of the best physical therapists at the rehab center, but they had a love/hate relationship with him. He was excellent when he and Alex were working, but an arrogant ass the rest of the time.

"I'm coming. Don't get your panties in a twist." Expecting him to wheel away, he winked instead and pulled her onto his lap for a kiss. It was the first time he'd initiated anything intimate since he'd been wounded, and it squeezed her heart in all the good places.

But when Carlos signed loudly, she couldn't hold back her giggle.

"You better go. He's going to torture you in there."

"Maybe, but Hunter will protect me. Right, boy?" Hunter woofed in response as she hopped off his lap. "Ciao, baby. See you after my session."

"I'll be waiting." She watched him roll into the building with Hunter by his side, then she grabbed her tablet and bag and followed him. She'd see if she could find Tag and get the details about the party and then try to get some work done.

❧ ❧ ❧

"Who's this?" Carlos asked as he waited for Alex to get to him.

"Hunter. He's a therapy dog."

"So, you finally got him, huh?"

"Did everyone know I was getting a dog except me?"

"Yup. Now hustle, we have a lot to do today, and you're wasting time."

Grumbling under his breath about impatient

asswipes, he followed Carlos to the torture chamber. If anyone ever tried to tell you that PT was great, they were either lying or never had to do it. It hurt like hell. Not that he was afraid of pain, but the pain without any progress was just pissing him the fuck off. In all fairness, he'd only been working with Carlos for a week, but he'd had months of therapy at Walter Reed before they got home.

"Dr. Andrews called this morning. You get to move up to the next level today."

"That means what exactly? More torture?"

"You know it." Just freakin' wonderful.

"Did he say anything else? X-ray results or anything?"

"Only that some of the swelling was down so we could work on some other areas to help keep you in shape. You can flap your lips with him at your appointment. Now it's time for work, bro." Hunter growled when Carlos approached him, and it surprised them both.

"What's wrong, boy? It's okay." He spoke in the low, soothing tone Cage showed him earlier. But Hunter wasn't backing down. He placed himself square in front of Alex and blocked Carlos from getting any closer.

"Tell your guard dog to chill."

"If you weren't such an asshole he'd be fine. But he picks up on attitude, and he probably thinks you're going to hurt me. He isn't wrong either, just not how he thinks."

"Do something about it." Alex considered not doing anything. But if Dr. Andrews said he was making progress then he needed to get his ass in gear.

"Hunter, he's a friend. He just acts like an ass."

"Ugh, gee thanks."

"It's true. Hold your hand out slowly. But don't try to touch him."

"Hunter. It's okay. See, he won't hurt me." Slowly the dog relaxed, and after one more low growl at Carlos, he moved back to the side of Alex's chair. "See it's all good."

"Except now you've wasted fifteen minutes. C'mon I'll show you the new machine we're going to be using today."

"Great. Hunter, stay." The dog didn't look like he wanted to listen, but he did, laying down on the floor where Alex pointed. The next forty-five minutes were going to be ugly.

Fifty minutes later, Alex was ready to dig a hole in the backyard and hibernate for the winter. He wasn't sure if it was having the training in the morning and then PT or if Carlos had just been that much harder on him. Probably a combination of both, plus the new machine. He had a feeling he'd be popping an extra pain pill before bed.

He couldn't wait to get away from the torture chamber, and went to look for Lily. Hunter saw her before he did. She was sitting in the waiting room and focused on something on her tablet. He should have known she'd be working. This new project was her biggest and most visible one yet and could take her little design firm into the big time if she handled it well. It was important to her, and he'd be her rock or something, but he'd be damned if they were going to treat her like shit either.

"Miss me, Lilybee?" He knew he startled her when she almost dropped the tablet and it took her eyes a second or two to focus on him.

"Hey, babe. Shit. Were you waiting long?"

"Nope. Just got done, but I am ready to get out the fuck out of dodge. How about you?"

"Yup. How did it go?"

"It was brutal. Abso-fucking-lutely brutal. But Dr. Andrews said the x-rays showed improvement, so he worked me harder. Progress, painful, but progress."

"Yay! That's great."

"Easy for you to say, you didn't just spend most of an hour in the room of horrors."

"True," she said with a giggle. "How about I treat you to Starbucks on the way home?" She looked so hopeful there was no way he'd say no. It was more her thing, after years in the field, just getting a cup of hot coffee was good enough. He didn't need any of that fancy shit to make him happy.

"Sure. Just get me out of here before Carlos decides he has some extra time. Thank God I have the weekend off."

"Yeah, about that. He's going to be at the party on Sunday too."

"Shit, really?"

"Yeah. I spoke to Tag about it while I was waiting for you." They'd gotten to the car, and as he lifted himself from the wheelchair to the car, the shooting pain made the world spin. Thankfully, Lily was too busy telling him about the party plans to notice, but Hunter did and put his head in his lap. Petting his furry head helped him to center himself, and work through the pain. He might have pushed a little too hard today. It was worth if it since he was finally making progress.

"Are you okay? You look a little pale," Lily said as she buckled her seatbelt. He turned to see her staring at him, her expression concerned.

"I'm fine. Just worn out. I think there may be a nap in my future. I never took one this morning."

"No wonder you were ready when I got downstairs earlier. I'd say a nap sounds like a wonderful idea."

"But first Starbucks. You could use an extra boost."

"I'm fine. I can make coffee at home."

"Nope. I could go for a slice of their gingerbread stuff. I bet Hunter will like it too."

"I'm sure he will." Asking for something guaranteed they'd stop, he knew his wife well. She played the tough snarky female but she was nothing but a big marshmallow in the inside, and everyone who knew her eventually figured it out.

CHAPTER 7

The weekend went quickly. Alex and Hunter spent most of the days together either walking or hanging out while Lily worked on the Walcott project. She was relieved that there hadn't been any incidents following the meeting, but couldn't shake the niggling feeling that something wasn't right.

The job was hers, that's what the boss said, so no matter what the asshole Chandler had to say, she had work to do. By Sunday afternoon she had a good plan for the opening roll out. It was a relief too, it meant she wouldn't worry about taking the night off for the Taggart Christmas party.

Neither she nor Alex were big partiers anymore, but she'd been looking forward to getting out and having some fun. It would be good for both of them—at least she hoped it would. And since they never went out, she'd decided to get dressed up for a change. She'd gone through her closet twice before settling on a forest green dress, low-cut enough to be sexy but not so much she'd have to wear a strapless or worry about a wardrobe malfunction. The biggest chore for her was the makeup. Other than mascara she was usually bare-faced. She went the whole nine yards, maybe even ten if she thought about it. After sliding the red lipstick across her bottom lip, she sat back and examined her reflection in the mirror.

Shit. She hardly recognized herself. It was like she'd had one of those makeovers. But all she'd done is gone on YouTube and learned how to do the 'smoky eye' technique, added some fake eyelashes, face makeup and blush. Then she completed the look with some bright red lipstick. It was brighter than she felt comfortable wearing usually, and she didn't even remember buying it, but it fit the flirty, sexy look she hoped would entice Alex. Satisfied with the final result, she stepped into a pair of black four-inch heels and prayed she wouldn't break her neck before the night was finished.

"You almost ready?" Alex called from the bottom of the stairs and looked up just as she'd started down, and his voice trailed off. The surprise quickly turned to admiration and then heat as his gaze slid down her body and took in every curve revealed by the clingy fabric of the dress. "Holy fuck. Yeah, I'd say you're ready."

The look on his face sent a thrill down her spine. Mission accomplished. She finally admitted that she'd been nervous about it. Especially after every attempt she'd made at intimacy had been rebuffed. But maybe tonight would be different, it was promising so far.

"Does that mean you approve?" she asked as she did a pirouette in the hallway. A wolf whistle from Alex and a woof from Hunter was the answer.

"Hell yeah. Shit woman, you're gonna be the death of me. Everyone is going to be drooling all over you. Maybe you should put on something a bit less…"

"Oh hell no. We haven't been out in ages, and I never get dressed up. I kind of like it." It was a half-truth. She was enjoying the fire in his eyes and the very prominent bulge in his pants, but maybe she'd gone a little over the top with the eyelashes. "Let me grab the wine, and we can go." As she walked into the dining room to get the bottle, she felt his eyes on her, and she couldn't resist adding an extra swing to her hips. His low groan made her smile with satisfaction. Yes, this little game of dress-up was a good idea.

Willow Haven was a small town, but even after living there for five years there was a lot she had never seen. Too much time in her PJs in front of the computer had its drawbacks for sure. Anna Taggart's house was one of those places. It was tucked away at the end of a neighborhood of large modern homes with lots of glass. Anna's was the same, but you couldn't see it from the street. Then she remembered that this was the first house in the development. A development built by her family.

"Nice place, huh?"

"No shit. I wonder what it looks like on the inside?"

"Park the car, Lilybee, and we'll find out." Lilybee. He hadn't called her that in longer than she could remember, and now it was twice in the last few days. Another little sign that her Alex was coming back.

"Smart ass."

"Some things never change." But some things do. She pulled around the circular drive, and a valet stepped up to open her door. "Seriously?" she whispered under her breath, but Alex heard and chuckled.

"I have to get a wheelchair out of the trunk," Lily said as she climbed out of the car.

"I'll get it for you, ma'am." Damn, there it was again. Stupid ma'am shit, and it didn't help that Alex was laughing his ass off inside the car.

The house was lit with Christmas lights, and there were two huge wreaths on double front doors. It looked like something out of House and Garden Magazine, and she suddenly was a whole lot happier that she'd gotten dressed up. One of the doors opened as they approached.

"Lily and Alex? Glad you could make it. Very glad, in fact now I win twenty bucks from Tag."

"What?"

"Shitheads. Both of you. Lily, this is Ethan. I don't think you've met him. He's Anna's pet police detective."

Lily laughed. "Nice to meet you, Ethan. I thought you looked familiar. You helped take down that burglary ring, right?"

"Yup, that would be me. My partner, Steele too. He's inside, along with half of Fitzsimmons Air Force Base, I think." He stepped back into the doorway to allow them access. "Nice dog. Tag's dog is here tonight too. Have you met Jackson yet?"

"Not yet, but I've heard plenty."

"I did last week. He's very fierce looking. Scared the shit out of me when I walked into Tag's office at the Rehab Center. I'd completely forgotten about him."

Lily had to stop herself from staring because inside Anna's home was even more beautiful—and filled with an enormous amount of people. Her introverted-self wanted to turn around and run for the car until she saw Chloe and Logan across the room.

While Ethan and Alex were talking, Lily went over to talk to Chloe and Logan. It wasn't until she got closer that she realized they were talking to Cage, the trainer from Paws for Hope and another guy who was at least two inches taller than him. What were they feeding these guys?

"Hi."

"Oh wow, Lily, you look amazing," Chloe

said as she hugged her. Logan gave her a hug too.

"Chloe's right. You clean up good, kid."

"Funny man. I figured why not, it's the holidays right?" Chloe laughed, before turning to Cage and his friend.

"I'd like you to meet my best friend, Lily Barrett. She's married to that hunk over there, the one next to the fluffy four-legged mutt."

"Hey, don't pick on Hunter like that. He's beautiful in his own way. But, I already know Cage. He's Alex and Hunter's trainer, right? Nice to see you again."

"That's cool. But do you know Chase Brennan?"

"Nope. Nice to meet you, Chase."

"Likewise, ma'am."

"Geesh. Do I look that old?"

Logan guffawed and almost spilled his drink. "Dork, we're all military or ex-military. It's just a habit. It doesn't bother Chloe."

"Speak for yourself," she said as she elbowed her husband in the side.

"You're having too much fun without me," Alex said as rolled up with Hunter as his wingman. "Hey, Cage. I didn't realize you were going to be here."

"You know how it is, we're really just one big family."

"Truth, that." Chase nodded.

"Alex, this is Chase, Chase Brennan. I told you about him the other day, remember?"

"Yeah. You run Eagle Security and Protection, or something like that, right?"

"Exactly. Although we just call it ESP, it's a whole lot easier."

That caught Lily's attention. Security and protection. Would they look into Harrison Chandler for her? She'd managed to keep his latest shit from Alex, but his harassing emails were getting more and more threatening. There'd been about fifteen since Friday. What bothered her more than the threats were the pictures of Alex and Hunter in the yard, and of her sitting at her desk. How the hell had he or his thug friends gotten close enough to take photos of her through her office window? Especially since it was on the second floor.

It freaked her the fuck out, but in classic Lily mode she had put it out of her mind and worked on the project. She needed the grand opening plans to be perfect. It was one of those career-changing projects. Although she was so busy already, she might have to think about getting an actual office and hiring a few people. But as her grandmother always said, 'don't put the cart before the horse.' Too bad all the crap from the asswipe was putting a damper on everything.

"Exactly. And I hear you've got skills on the computer too, Alex." What? She must have gone off in her own world because she had no idea what they were talking about. And since when did Alex have mad computer skills?

"Yeah. Haven't had much use for them lately, though."

"What's your status?"

"Still in medical eval hell. I'm pretty much assured of a medical discharge if I want it. I just wasn't sure it was the way I wanted to go." At least this part she knew. They'd talked about it a bit in the hospital, and then some more yesterday. But the computer stuff was new to her.

"Maybe you should come by our office. Check it out. You might decide you'd like to come work with us. I like to keep it in the family, although you'd be our first Ranger. Probably get a lot of crap from the other SEALs."

"Very funny," Logan cut in. "You guys are a

laugh riot. We can take you any day of the week."

"Hey bro, shut the hell up. I can't do much damage from this chair. Give me a few months at least."

The women shrugged and rolled their eyes at each other. It was the same every time a group of them got together. Like a bunch of teenage boys hanging out in the bathroom bragging about who had the biggest dick. Would they ever grow up? Unlikely. But then again, did they want them to?

"C'mon girl. Let's leave the guys to talk shop. I need a drink. My breasts have finally been liberated from the child." Chloe grabbed Lily's arm and pulled her away from the testosterone four-pack.

"All right! Although I'm driving. Only one glass of wine for me."

"Let's make it a good one then. Screw the wine, let's have a peach Bellini. I haven't had one of those in ages." Lily agreed, and they navigated through the crowd toward the bar.

"Chloe, Lily, right? I'm so glad you came. Are you having a good time?" Their hostess, Anna Taggart, was tall, thin, and gorgeous, and Tag's younger sister. She ran Willow Haven

Realty now that her parents were retired and traveled constantly. Lily knew she'd wanted Tag to work with her, but he'd turned her down. He had a rough adjustment after he was wounded and had left town for almost a year.

It had driven his girlfriend, Julie, crazy when he didn't tell her where he'd gone. It really was a small town. Now that Lily thought about it, she knew way more than she realized about a lot of the people at the party. Like Chase said earlier, they were like one huge family.

"Thank you for inviting us. Your home is beautiful." Lily called Chloe Ms. Manners for just this reason. She always knew the perfect thing to say. While Lily stood there with a dumb ass smile on her face.

"Thank you. It's a work in progress now that Ethan has moved in." A tinge of a rose colored her cheeks as she gazed across the room at her boyfriend. Scratch that, fiancé if the huge ring on her hand was any indication.

"How is Alex's dog working out?"

"Hunter is wonderful. I can't believe how much he's helped Alex, even after only a few days."

Anna nodded. "It was the same I think for

Tag. When he and Jackson got back from Montana, he was a new man. He says it's all because of Jackson. It's like having to care for the dogs gives them a feeling of worth, besides the support the dogs give back."

"That's true. I hadn't thought about it that way. Whatever it is, I can't thank Tag and Logan enough for setting it up for him. I would never have thought about it."

"I know. I thank God that the people at the Montana rehab ranch introduced Tag and Jackson. I really think we might have lost him otherwise. His PTSD and depression were so much worse than he ever let on. Even Mac hadn't realized, and they were living together."

"Really? That's so scary. Alex is still having horrible nightmares, although Hunter definitely does a better job soothing him than I did."

"Logan has them too. Although the longer he's home, the better he seems to be getting. The other night I woke up, and he wasn't in bed, I freaked out. But he was in Andy's room sitting in the rocking chair, cuddling Andy in his arms and talking. I didn't want to intrude, but it looked like quite a deep conversation."

"That's so sweet," Anna said with a smile.

"Yeah, it was. I didn't let him know I saw,

but I was really curious about what they were talking about."

"Hey, sexy," Ethan said as he pulled Anna close and gave her a kiss. "I hate to steal her away from you, but the caterers are having an issue in the kitchen."

"Seriously? Oops. I'll catch up with you later. Or maybe we can all get together for lunch next week?"

"Sounds good."

"She is very nice," Chloe remarked as they continued their trek to the bar and got their drinks. When Lily looked around for Alex, she didn't see him or Hunter anywhere. Or Logan either for that matter.

"I wonder where our guys went?"

"I'm sure they're talking shop. I know Logan misses being in the middle of things. He doesn't say it, but he gets a look every so often."

"Do you think he'll volunteer for another deployment?"

"No. If it hadn't been for Andy and Alex, maybe. But Andy's birth and Alex getting wounded he changed. He said that family was more important than his career. He's been talking to Chase about their business too. I don't think he's decided yet on whether to put in for early retirement."

"Alex doesn't want to leave. I think it validates him. But he can't go back to the kind of life he had, even when he is able to walk again."

"Maybe he'll take Chase up on his offer?"

"I didn't even know he was good with the computer. Did Logan talk to you about what he did over there?"

"Nope. It's all the hush-hush if I tell you I'll have to kill you shit. I stopped asking a long time ago."

"Me too. I didn't even think about it. It's weird now to get little insights into what was going on."

Chloe nodded as she took a sip of her Bellini. "Have you talked to Beth or Julie since you got back?"

"No, I haven't. This week has been totally insane. None stop running around. I haven't had time for much else besides work and Alex."

"I'm so glad you're back. I missed you. Speaking of work, what's going on with the asshole at Walcott?"

"Shit, we were having such a good time too. You had to bring it up?"

"Well, what are best friends for?"

"Brat!"

"You're not going to put me off that easily. I'm a mom, remember? I have the power to weasel it out of you."

Lily laughed. She'd seen Chloe in action with Lexie and Bella. Hell, she didn't stand a chance. "Fine. But it's not a big deal. Only some emails."

"You're holding something back. I can tell. C'mon, fess up."

"You are a pain in the ass, you know?"

"Yeah, yeah, but you love me. Quit stalling."

"He's sent a lot of emails since Friday when I saw him. But they're just emails. What's bugging me a bit, or would if I had time to think about it, are the pictures."

"What pictures?"

"Yeah, what pictures?" Shit, when had Alex and Logan come up behind them? And why didn't Chloe warn her? Ugh, because she wanted them to know. Damn.

"It's nothing, babe."

"Don't. Logan told me about Chandler."

"How? Shit. I thought you were going to keep my secret?" Lily felt a little better when Chloe looked embarrassed.

"I was going to, but then I started to think about what he'd said. I'm worried about you. I can't keep stuff I'm worried about from Logan or you. You know that."

"Yeah." And she did. She should have realized nothing stayed a secret for long.

"Tell me, baby. What's going on now?"

"Just some emails, and pictures of you and Hunter in the yard and me at my desk." Before she could finish, he cut her off.

"At your desk? In our house? What the fuck?"

"Shh. We're at a party remember? I don't need everyone knowing our business. Err my business."

"Actually, maybe we do. What do you know about this Chandler guy? And we're going to have a talk about this when we get back home. You should know better than to keep stuff like this from me. No secrets—that was our promise from the beginning. Or don't you remember?"

"I remember." Lily wasn't sorry she'd kept it from him, though. He'd been dealing with so much, and she refused to believe Chandler was a real threat. It was Willow Haven; the biggest thing to happen in their sleepy town was the burglary ring.

"Logan, what do you think? Maybe we should bring Chase in on this and see what he has to say?"

"Wait. Do you really want to involve more people? It's probably nothing at all and Chandler is just full of shit."

"That's true, he might be, but I'm not taking that chance with my wife. Your protection is my responsibility." And if she didn't already get the idea, Hunter woofed in agreement.

CHAPTER 8

It was after midnight when Lily and Alex got home. He was tired, but for the first time since he'd been wounded, he had a purpose. They talked to Chase and Cage, who he found out worked for ESP and only did the training with Paw for Hope between cases. Tomorrow he and Lily would bring her laptop and go over to the ESP offices to discuss everything in detail.

He was happy they'd gone, even though up until Lily had come downstairs looking like sex on a stick, he'd been dreading it. One look at her in that dress and he'd have followed her to the ends of the Earth. Holy sheep shit, Batman. Not that he didn't love her in PJs and fuzzy slippers because he did. She was his Lilybee.

But tonight, she looked more like she'd been ready for a photo shoot. He was glad she hadn't gone to her meeting dressed that way or he might have even more shit to deal with.

Chandler was the one who seemed to be causing all the trouble, but Alex wasn't too happy about Walcott either. There was something fishy about this whole thing. He hadn't said anything to Lily about it, but he'd been doing some research on his own, and there was a bunch of shit that didn't add up.

After Hunter had done his business outside, he wheeled into the kitchen. Lily was fiddling with her phone. "Something wrong?"

She jumped then turned toward him. A guilty look on her face. "Nope, nothing at all."

"And you think I'll buy that?" With a shake of her head, she walked over to show him her phone. He took it from her and read the threatening email. The timestamp was only a half hour earlier. What the fuck was this asshole thinking? Didn't he realize who he was dealing with?

"Bitch, don't make me tell you again. You need to walk away now.

You have no idea who you're pissing off. If you don't want your crippled man to pay for your stupidity, you'll do as we say."

"It'll be okay, baby. I swear. He won't touch any of us."

"I know. I still think he's full of shit. But the thugs he was arguing with in the parking lot? I'm not so sure about them."

"What? Why is this the first I'm hearing about them?"

"C'mon we've been over this. You had enough shit going on. I have been taking care of myself while you were gone. It's not like I had you to run to with every problem. I'm pretty self-sufficient, you know."

"I do know. But you don't have to be now. That's all I'm saying. Tell me about the thugs."

"Actually, I had something else in mind." Fuck. He was in trouble now. He knew that look, and her voice was huskier. His dick knew it too, and he came right to attention. "I have an idea. I know you're in pain."

"Not so much right now…"

"Shh. Let me finish. I thought that maybe we could try it while you're in the chair."

"What?" She was losing her mind for sure. But the more he thought about it, the more turned on he got. It just might work. He'd have the leverage from the chair. But before he could say or do anything, she'd stepped closer.

"How about we take this into the other room?" He followed her into the living room. She'd lit a bunch of candles and put on some music while he was outside with Hunter. With only the light of the flickering candles, he had no doubt that she was trying to seduce him. He tried to hide his grin while talking to Hunter.

"Hey, boy. Go lay down in your bed. I'll call you if I need you." The dog hesitated for a moment and then did as he'd asked. "What did you have in mind?"

"Are you willing to try? Or are you going to lose it like the last time." Even in the dim light, he could see the flash of pain on her face. He hadn't meant to hurt her, but he couldn't be the man she needed. He wasn't sure he could tonight, either. But he needed to try—for both of them.

"Yes. Now come closer." Her smile dripped pure sex. He tensed, waiting for the inevitable pain his hard-on triggered, but it didn't happen. The only pain he had was from the zipper digging in to his flesh where it tried to get free. He didn't think he could get any harder, but he was wrong.

Instead of coming over, she reached behind her back as she unzipped her dress and let it slowly drop to the floor revealing the sexiest lingerie he'd ever seen on his wife. "Holy fuck, Lily. You're going to be the death of me."

"Maybe. But what a way to go."

He thanked God he hadn't known what was under the dress all night because they'd never have left the house. Slowly, way too slowly, torturing him with her small steps, each time getting just a bit closer, but still out of his reach.

Staring at his wife, he groaned. Her pale skin was illuminated by the flickering candlelight. She was so beautiful. His eyes were drawn to the black lace bra that barely contained her large breasts. How he'd fantasized about sucking on them, tonguing them, nipping at her hard nipples. But he hadn't touched her in almost a whole year. That needed to change and now. His eyes continued down, over her slightly rounded belly, to the lace bikini panties and thigh highs. His wife had turned into a sex kitten before his eyes.

With a growl, he reached for her, but she

was still beyond his reach. "Come to me."

She didn't answer. Instead, her tongue slid across her ruby-red lips, and she smiled. Pure sex. Damn, he needed her. Now. If his erection got any bigger, he'd bust through his pants. He was sure of that.

Finally, she was in front of him. He reached for her, but she batted his hands away. Yup, she was trying to kill him. Her fingers slid over his erection, taunting him, and he got even harder. Just when he thought he couldn't take anymore, she unbuttoned and unzipped his fly, releasing him. All eight inches of hot, thick, male twitched under her gaze, and as she licked her lips again a little bead of moisture formed at the tip. He couldn't hold back his groan, and he'd tried.

He wanted control, and she denied it. He'd never been so turned on. Desperate to touch her, taste her, take her into his arms and fill her full. "Don't make me beg."

"Mmmm, I think that's a great idea. You deserve it after making me wait." Her words said one thing, but her fingers slid up and down his length and rubbed the moisture into this skin. He was trying to hold back, but it had been so long since he'd felt her skin on his, her touch. It was taking all of his willpower not to lose control.

"Baby, please. I can't hold on much longer." He hoped she'd give in. Let him feel her too. Instead, she kneeled and slowly took him between those bright red lips. It was too much. He tried to pull away, but she held on tight. One hand fondled his balls while the other held the base of his shaft as she worked her magic, taking him deep.

He struggled to hold on, it was too fast, he wanted to please her. It should be her not him finding release.

"Oh, baby. If you don't want it, you need to stop now. I can't. Oh God."

But she wouldn't stop, and with one more squeeze, he lost control, shooting down her throat. He watched the muscles of her neck work as she swallowed every bit, and then she licked him clean.

It was impossible, but somehow, he was still hard. Is this what abstinence did to him? Shit. He throbbed. He wanted to get up out of the chair and toss her onto the couch. To make long slow love to her until she screamed his name.

"I see you're ready for more." He couldn't deny it; the proof was standing straight up in his lap. This hadn't happened since he was in his early twenties, but he wasn't going to complain. He wanted her. Needed to be buried deep inside her.

"Haven't you tortured me enough? I need to touch you." He didn't think she'd give in, but then she hopped up onto the arms of the wheelchair and balanced her legs over the sides. Her hot center hovered over him. If he could just thrust, he could get inside her. But she pressed down on his shoulders and slid her heat along his hardness covering him in her juices. That's when he realized her panties were crotchless. Holy fuckin' mother of God. She was killing him but what a way to go.

Reaching around her back, he unhooked her bra and let her beautiful breasts free. He cupped one in his hand and tweaked her hard nipple. Now it was her turn to groan, as she wriggled against his hard cock.

"Oh, babe. I've missed you."

"I know. I'm sorry, my love. You deserve…"

"Shhh…" She cut him off with her lips. His tongue pushed into her mouth, dueling with hers. He could taste himself, but it didn't bother him. She was his, all his. He'd been stupid, but he'd make it up to her.

Lifting her breast, he bent his head and took her rose-colored nipple between his lips and sucked. She squirmed. He sucked harder. Her juices dripped onto him, and he couldn't wait. He had to have her.

She must have read his mind because she readjusted her legs on the arms of the wheelchair and lowered herself over him. He leaned back and watched as her body sucked him in just as she'd done with her lips. Fuck.

He tilted his hips, not much, but enough to hit the spot he knew would send her over the edge. His balls tightened, and he wouldn't be able to hold off for long. Her rhythm grew choppy as he lifted enough so each time she came down on him, he hit her G-spot.

Her muscles clenched around him, her breathing grew ragged. Their combined juices slid down his shaft. A few more thrusts. She was so close. He tightened his hips and thrust up once, and again.

She screamed his name. Her body quivering against his, tears in her eyes. "I love you, Alex. You are my world."

"You reminded me what it means to be alive. You are and always will be the love of my life. Thank you, baby."

CHAPTER 9

They'd planned to go to the Eagle Security & Protection Agency offices after breakfast. While they had their coffee, Lily got a strange email from Enid Mercier, Walcott's assistant. There was no message, only an attachment, and he wouldn't let her open it. He didn't want her to take any chances. It also ensured they'd be visiting ESP first thing. He called Cage and let him know he might be late for his training session with Hunter.

Neither of them discussed the night before, but for the first time since coming back home he didn't feel anxious, and he hadn't had a nightmare either. He'd woken up refreshed, even though they'd only had a few hours of sleep. She'd even slept in his bed. He figured Hunter was jealous since somewhere in the middle of the night he'd been growling. But eventually, he settled down.

It gave him hope for the future and how they'd deal with things if he couldn't walk again. Maybe it wouldn't be as black as he'd thought. And thanks to Chase there was the possibility of a job outside of the Army. Something he'd never contemplated before.

As they drank their coffee, he questioned her about the Walcott project. She didn't know as much as he'd hoped. She'd only been involved for a week. Construction was mostly done, only finishing touches on the fitness center and decorating of the restaurant and spa were still needed. Which is why Walcott needed Lily. She was the best at what she did, even if it wasn't well known. He also asked her to describe the guys in the parking lot who'd been with Chandler. He wanted a good idea of what they looked like so he could watch for them. He didn't believe they wouldn't try something, not after going through the effort to send the pictures. They meant business. But so did he. There was no way they'd touch a hair on his wife's head.

After they had finished their coffee, Lily

went upstairs to pack her notes and get the laptop. He took Hunter outside for a quick walk in the backyard, then walked around to the front of the house to wait near the car for her. That's when he noticed all four tires on their card had been slashed. Fuck. They weren't going anywhere in that now. He didn't need to be a rocket scientist to figure out who was behind it. Now Hunter's growling in the middle of the night made a lot more sense. "Thanks, buddy. I should have listened better. I'm sorry." The dog woofed and rubbed against him as he pulled his phone out of his pocket and dialed nine-one-one.

The kitchen door opened, and Lily stepped onto the driveway as he disconnected his call. She was more observant than him and noticed the tires right away. He hadn't seen them until he'd rolled up to the passenger door.

"What the fuck happened?"

"My guess is we had a visit from your 'thugs.'"

"Dammit."

"It's okay. I called the police, and they're on their way. It helps when you have friends in the department. I also called Chase. He's coming too."

"This screws with everything."

"It'll be fine. Seriously." He wheeled toward her as the surprise turned to anger and then fear. "Lilybee, look at me. Baby." Finally, she stopped staring at the car and met his eyes. "You're safe. I won't let anything happen to you."

"I don't understand any of this. It's a freaking design job. How can that make someone so upset that they threaten us?"

"I don't know. But we're going to find out. Why don't you go inside and see if you can do some work? Or call Chloe. But try to get your mind off this. I'll wait out here for the police and Chase."

"Okay." He lifted her hand and kissed her palm. She smiled and leaned down to kiss him. If they hadn't been on the driveway, he'd have pulled her into his lap and kissed her senseless.

"Hey, get a room you two." And this is why a driveway seduction is never a good idea.

"Shit, Chase, how did you get here so fast?"

"That's my secret."

"Hi, Chase. I bet you didn't expect this." Chase was smart and observant and picked up on Lily's fear right away.

"Nope but it's not the worst way to start a

week. I love a mystery. But I'd love a cup of coffee if you could manage it. I didn't have a chance to stop yet."

"Oh sure. Alex, would you like one too?"

"Yes, thanks." After she'd gone back inside, Chase started his questions.

"Don't you want to wait for the cops?"

"Nope. They'll be looking for the perps who did this, we're looking for the why behind it."

"It doesn't make any sense. Lily is a graphic designer and marketing specialist. Why the hell would that trigger this shit?"

"I don't know, but I'd say somehow your wife is in the middle of something much bigger."

"Yeah, no shit Sherlock. That's the understatement of the year."

"I like you more and more, Alex. I think you'll make a good addition to the team. I really hope you'll consider my offer."

"I am. At least it'll be more interesting than pushing papers behind a desk for the Army. I'm sure as hell not into teaching like Logan's doing. He can keep that shit."

Chase laughed. "I hear that." He took out his phone and snapped some pictures of the car from all sides, and a couple of close-ups of the slashes in the tires. He was finishing up when Lily was back with two steaming mugs of coffee. A car pulled up, and Ethan and Steele climbed out. The police had arrived.

"Nice way to start a Monday, huh?" Ethan said as he walked around the car. Steele shook hands with Alex.

"You think this is connected to what we were talking about last night?"

"Hell yeah." Then Alex looked up and saw Lily getting that scared rabbit look again. "Hey baby, I'll take that coffee now."

"Oh shit. Sorry. I didn't realize…" Her words trailed off, but he knew she was beating herself up for something. Typical Lilybee.

"No worries. It won't be too hot to drink now."

"Jerk." Good, the response he was looking for.

"You guys want some coffee?"

"No thanks, I'm good. Ethan?"

"Thanks anyway, but I had half a pot already. Some of us work for a living."

"You're a funny guy, Ethan. Good thing you're my brother's partner or I might have to kick your ass and show you how the SEALs do it. I already ran ten miles this morning and spent an hour in the gym. Once a SEAL always a SEAL."

"If y'all are done with your pissing contest and don't need me anymore, I'm going inside. I have work to do, at least until something else happens."

"Sorry, Lily."

"It's okay. I know you're not serious and would give up your lives for each other in a heartbeat."

"Damn straight. Chloe, Anna, Beth, and Julie too. Once you're with one of us you're with all of us."

Alex spewed his coffee across the driveway.

Lily laughed too. "I know you don't mean that the way it sounded. And thank you. You all rock. Let me know if you need anything."

After she had gone back inside, Alex looked Chase up and down. "You really ran ten miles this morning?"

"Every day. I might not be active duty, but I can't seem to break the habit. Too many years. Besides, it keeps me ready for whatever comes up, and we've had a few cases that were just as dangerous as a mission. Ask Cage about Costa Rica some time. He'll tell you."

"Okay, so how do you want to handle this?"

Steele asked. As he snapped a couple of pictures. Between all of them, there was no way they'd missed a thing. Gotta love technology.

"You guys file the police report. Unless there is something here that leads us back to Harrison Chandler, we can't pin it on him. I'll go back to the office and see what kind of dirt I can dig up on him and Walcott for that matter."

"Oh yeah, this morning his assistant sent Lily a file attachment. No message just the file. I wouldn't let her open it."

"Good idea. You guys finish up here, and I'll go in and see what's on that file."

"You're not our boss or CO, dick. We know how to do our jobs."

"Then why are you standing there?"

"Fucking family," Steele grumbled, but his words were softened by the grin on his face. "We'll be done in a few."

Alex and Hunter, who'd been laying on the driveway by his side through all of the commotion, went inside with Chase. Lily was sitting at the kitchen table on her laptop with another cup of coffee. Her gaze was transfixed on the screen. He had a bad feeling. The hairs on the back of his neck stood up as he wheeled closer to look over his wife's shoulder.

Instead of going up to her office, Lily set the laptop on the kitchen table and got another cup of coffee. Coffee was the one constant in her life, a soothing elixir of yummy. Her go to cup of comfort no matter what. In college, it had been wine, but now she'd rather drink a pot of coffee than a bottle of wine. Her father had been an alcoholic. Remembering him hiding in the garage with his bottle of whiskey was a big deterrent to drinking alone, and since Alex was gone more than home she was happy to stick to her coffee high.

As usual, the first thing she did was check her email. It was another habit. Without thinking, she clicked on the email from Enid and opened the attachment. Cringing when she remembered she'd promised Alex she wouldn't open it. A video started loading, still on autopilot, she raised the volume. What she saw next took her breath away.

When it finished buffering the screen was almost black. She could just make out a shadowed figure. Then she heard the voice. It wasn't

Chandler either. This was menacing and raised goosebumps on her arms.

"This is what happens to people who don't mind their own business. Or get involved in something they shouldn't. You didn't listen. You're next, bitch!" The camera moved and focused on a slumped figure tied to a chair.

Alex touched her shoulder. She screeched and nearly jumped out of her chair. "Holy shit, you scared the crap out of me."

"Didn't I tell you not to open that file?"

"I didn't mean to."

"Sure." While they were talking, she'd never taken her eyes off the screen. As the person came into focus, she realized it was Enid Mercier. "Oh my God. Fuck, it's Enid." Alex wheeled closer and put his arm around her.

She wanted to look away from the screen but she couldn't. It was like driving past a train wreck and not stopping to look. Was she still alive? Could they save her?

"I don't know." Lily didn't realize she'd asked the question out loud. "Chase, what do you think?"

"I can't tell, he's not close enough. Let's go to my office. We can analyze it on the high-tech equipment we have there."

The entire time the camera was focused on Enid she hadn't made a sound, hadn't moved. What looked like blood was pooled at her feet. Then the shadowed figure walked into the frame and pulled her head up by her hair. She'd been beaten. Although the word beaten wasn't even close to describing what happened to the poor woman. Lily barely recognized her. She'd been so perfect when she'd seen her on Friday. One of her eyes was swollen closed, her face covered with blood and black bruises. Her clothes had been sliced open, and bloody wounds covered her chest. But what scared Lily the most was the one eye that stared into the camera—unseeing. She had her answer. Enid Mercier was dead. His words echoed in her brain. They were coming for her next.

The room started to spin, and she couldn't catch her breath.

"Baby. Lily, look at me," Alex pleaded. But she couldn't stop staring at the laptop screen. A hand reached past her face and shut the lid. Even when she closed her eyes, she couldn't get the sight out of her mind. Would she ever? Then she remembered the old saying, "what is seen cannot be unseen." It couldn't be real, could it?

"Lily!" Alex's voice sounded desperate through the fog of her brain. Then he shook her, at least she thought it was him. Slowly she turned to face him. "There you are. Listen to me. This could all just be a set up to scare you."

"You think so?" She hoped and prayed. But deep in her gut, she knew it was all too real, and Enid Mercier wouldn't see another day.

"I hate to ask this, Lily, but does that room look familiar to you at all?" She'd forgotten Chase was there. Apparently at some point during the video, Ethan and Steele had come in too.

"No, not really. But it is dark. I'm sorry."

Chase turned to Ethan. "I'm going to take them back to the office. I'll send you a copy of the video when we get there. If it is what I think it is, it's a crime scene." Apparently, Chase thought it was real too. It didn't make her feel any better. She didn't even realize she was crying until Alex wiped her cheek. She didn't know much about Enid. Did she have a husband? Children? Was someone missing her right now?

"We'll find out, Lily. I promise you. We'll find the people responsible too." Lily was surprised she'd spoken her thoughts out loud again. Her inner dialogue must be broken.

"C'mon let's get you out of here."

"We'll let you know if we find anything," Steele said as he and Ethan headed out the door. That's when she noticed that Hunter was pacing back and forth across the kitchen. He must have been picking up on their stress.

"Hunter. C'mere, boy." She wasn't sure he'd come to her. He wasn't her dog after all. But he did and even laid his head in her lap. Running her fingers through his fluffy hair was more soothing than she'd expected. It made Alex's changes since getting Hunter even more understandable.

Alex grabbed the laptop and shoved it in her tote. "C'mon, baby. Time to go." She nodded and followed him to the door. Moving in a haze of horror as the scene on the video replayed over and over in her mind, the menace in the man's voice, echoing in her head. "You're next, bitch!"

CHAPTER 10

The ride to the Eagle Security & Protection's offices was a blur. At some point, she'd started shaking. She vaguely heard Alex tell Chase she was going into shock. Shock? It that what this was? So cold. Her teeth were chattering.

They were in Chase's office, but she didn't remember getting there. He walked through the door carrying a blanket and handed it to Alex. He draped it over her shoulders and then pulled her into his lap. Finally, she wasn't shivering as much. A glass was pushed against her lips. Alex's voice sounded far away when he encouraged her to take a drink. But she listened.

The liquid burned as it hit her throat and she choked. It did the trick. The warmth of the scotch spread through her body, thawing her in a way nothing else could.

"Better?"

"Yes. Thank you." She should sit in her own chair, but Alex's lap felt so warm. And safe. Safe was good. She needed safe right now. It would be okay to stay there for a few minutes, right?

"Lily, do you feel up to answering a few questions?"

"I think so. I don't know. I'll try."

"Do you want another swig of scotch, Lilybee?" Just hearing him say her nickname was comforting. She'd forgotten how much she'd missed it over the last few months. Damn, even her inner thoughts were rambling. Focus, Lily. You can do this.

"No, thank you. I'm good." She wasn't but maybe if she said it often enough she would be.

"Are you sure it was Enid Mercier? She's Walcott's assistant, right?"

"Yes, she is, was, and yes, I'm sure. She was wearing that suit when I saw her on Friday." She shuddered, the horror still front and center in her brain.

"Okay. This is probably the last thing you want to do but focus on the voice on the video. Did anything about it sound familiar?"

"No."

"Take a moment and focus."

"Babe, I know it's hard, but try. I'm here with you, you're safe." His arms held her a little closer. She closed her eyes and tried to concentrate on the voice. Deep, gravely and dripping with hatred. Had she heard it before?

"I don't think so. Well, maybe. No. Shit. I don't know. It kind of sounded like one of the guys yelling at Chandler in the Walcott parking lot. But I'm not really sure. I wasn't close enough to hear them clearly, just what carried over to me."

"Okay. Did you get a good look at any of them? If you saw any of them again would you recognize them.? I can have Ethan or Steele bring over a book of mugshots."

"I'm not sure. I mostly noticed Chandler. Can't you pick him up and make him tell you."

"We're not the police, we can't 'pick up anyone,' but I could have a talk with him if we could find him. Terrence Walcott seems to be missing too. Neither of them are at their homes or answering their cell phones. They didn't show up for work today either."

"You found all of this out already?"

"I told you we were good. This is what we do. I have a couple of the guys on it. If they're in Willow Haven, we'll find them."

"Okay. I guess it was too much to hope for that this could be resolved easily."

Warm at least, she pulled out of Alex's arms. It was time to pull up her big girl panties. She could handle this. She was the tough one. Settled in a chair next to Alex and across the desk from Chase. Almost immediately she missed the warmth of her husband's arms. Maybe they could sit on the couch and snuggle later? Focus, Lily. Her thoughts were never so disjointed. Was it a result of the shock? How long would it last? Shit, Chase was talking to her.

"I'm sorry, could you repeat what you said?"

"Sure. Lily, I'm sorry you're going through this, but you're not alone. Remember what I said. You're one of us. Have been since you married into the 'family,' you just haven't needed us until now."

Nodding she crossed her arms over her chest, feeling the chills starting again. "Thank you. But I have always been able to take care of myself. Ask Alex."

"I don't have to. He bitched about it enough last night." Chase chuckled, it was a comforting sound. Low, rumbling, and happy, and the opposite of the voice on the video.

His cell rang, and he held up his hand to stop what she was going to say next. "Brennan. Yup. Gotcha. No, not yet. Good, thanks. See you soon."

"That was Steele. They found signs of a struggle in Enid's office. And both her and Walcott's office had been trashed. They're figuring it had to be Chandler since security is so tight in that building. If not him, someone else on the inside."

"What kind of a business are they running? I know construction can be related to the mob, but this is Willow Haven. The boring elbow of Florida. Nothing happens here."

"Don't say that to Ethan. You weren't here when Anna was kidnapped, and he had to bust the burglary ring. It's not the quaint little beach town it once was."

"I guess not. So, what's next?"

"You and I are going in the tech area and see if we can get a match with facial recognition. I don't expect to, he made sure he was in the shadows the whole time. But if we're lucky it might be possible, or at the least maybe we can get him from his voice. You'd be surprised what we can do now."

"No, I wouldn't actually. I used a lot of that equipment."

"It's like that, huh?"

"Yeah. It is. And not anything I can discuss either. You know the routine."

"Me too. I know that routine all too well. What am I supposed to do while you two are off computer sleuthing?" Sounding coherent for the first time since she'd gotten to Chase's office, she surprised them. It was obvious from the looks on their faces.

"I can set you up in the conference room if you want to try to do some work. Do you have something other than the Walcott's stuff? I'm not sure what's going to happen with any of his holdings by the time this investigation is completed. You may not want to waste the time."

She hadn't thought about that. Shit. Oh well.

It wasn't toast yet, maybe all of this could work out somehow. Fuck. Who was she kidding? It was a ginormous clusterfuck squared. Luckily, she did have a few other customers who'd sent some work her way. She might as well get it done.

"Okay, I can do that. Thanks. If I don't do something besides sit here, I'm going to lose my mind."

Alex leaned over, kissed her forehead, and whispered, "It'll be okay. I promise, Lilybee. You'll see." She followed them out of Chase's office and down the hall to the conference room all the while praying he was right.

~~*~*

Alex and Hunter followed Chase further down the hallway after dropping Lily off in the conference room. He wasn't thrilled about leaving her there alone, but he doubted anything could happen to her at ESP. Chase was right, it was much easier to think of it as an acronym than the whole name, and ESP was kind of cool too.

Stopping in front of a door, Chase typed in a

keycode and led him into a room that rivaled any command center he'd ever been in.

"Okay Ranger man, show me your mad skills. Rock will set you up on a system."

"Rock?"

"Yeah. Don't ask, he'll rip off your head."

"Gotcha." Alex looked at the man sitting at one of the computers. At his name, Rock turned around. Shit. The man was huge. He should have been called mountain instead of rock. He came over to shake Alex's hand.

"Good to meet you, sir. I've heard a lot about you."

"No reason for the sir here. Alex is fine, uhhh Rock, is it?"

"Yup. Okay, I've got you all coded in here. I uploaded the video into the system and started running the recognition programs." He handed him a small piece of paper with Alex's password. "Memorize it."

That was nothing new for Alex. He wasn't worried, though. He had a photographic memory and passwords were cake for him, although this was a little more complicated than his usual. "Got it."

Rock took the paper and tossed it into an astray and lit it on fire.

"I guess I'm fucked if I forget it, huh?"

Chase howled with laughter from behind him. "Enough, Rock. If this were any other case, I'd say go for it, but it's his wife."

"You fuckers. You had me going."

"Well, that really was your password. But if you forget it I can get you back in," Rock said with a grin, flashing large white teeth that reminded him of the big bad wolf from Red Riding Hood, and he liked him right away. If he took the job after all of this was done, he'd have a team to work with again, and he had missed that.

Taking his place at the workstation, Alex's hands flew over the keys. He'd missed this, too. The thrill of the hunt. Then he remembered who they were hunting. The stakes were much different this time. He'd been on his share of rescue missions and a few others he didn't even want to think about. Most turned out fine, but he and Logan had been in their share of clusterfucks too. Mostly because of bad intel. It had been the main reason he'd taken the extra training. He'd never been sorry either.

He pulled up the video and messed with the contrast, noise and was able to get a slightly better image of the asshole threatening his wife.

"Shit. You're good. I've been messing with it for the last forty-five minutes, and I couldn't get it that clear," Rock said with awe.

"Not bad at all. I guess you do know what you're doing." Chase laughed when Alex gave him the finger over his shoulder. With Hunter lying by his feet and his fingers at home on the computer keys he felt useful for the first time since he'd been blown halfway across the base. The explosion had changed him in more ways than physically, and that had been the hardest part to deal with. Maybe taking this job was what he needed.

The program was running the facial recognition on the updated picture Alex fed it. Now it was a waiting game. It could happen fast or three days from now, or never. It all depended on whether the guy was in the system. The voice was even harder, and Alex suspected that he'd used some kind of a modulator to disguise it on the video. He obviously was into scare tactics.

He was good, managed to cover his digital trail pretty well, but Alex was better. After digging around in the metadata, Alex was able to find the asshole's first mistake. Now they knew where the video was shot and after a little back tracing, they got a location. Chase put a call into Steele, and he and Ethan were on their way to check it out. It was probably too much to hope that they'd find the asshole there and finish it all at one time.

They didn't want to tell Lily until they knew for sure one way or the other about Enid's condition. He'd never seen her like that, but it gave him a pretty good idea of how she'd been when she found out he was wounded. Logan had explained it to him, but seeing it first hand was heart wrenching. To know he'd put her though all of that. He'd find a way to make it up to her.

But for now, it was just a waiting game. Would Enid Mercier be alive? Would there be any hints to the location of Chandler or Walcott, and would they find anything to help figure out what or who was behind all of this?

Rather than wait in the command center, Alex told Chase he wanted to be with Lily. He wanted to be there when she heard the news good or bad. He hadn't decided if he wanted to tell her they'd figured out the location or not. He was leaning towards not, so she wouldn't sit and dwell on it until they had more information.

In the end, it didn't matter. When he and Chase got to the conference room, it was empty. Where the fuck was his wife? And why hadn't she texted or called to tell him she was leaving?

CHAPTER 11

After Alex and Chase had gone off on their bad guy hunt, Lily had pulled out her laptop and started working on an ad campaign for a local cupcake store. Their cupcakes were freakin' amazing, but they weren't getting the traffic they wanted or needed to pay their rent. Lily had a few ideas up her sleeve to help them generate more business than they could ever want.

Deep in design heaven, she was playing with different images of the cupcakes she'd taken before she'd gone to Maryland to be with Alex. Photoshop was one of her favorite programs. Making new pretty things always made her feel better. Sometimes she wondered why she took on all the marketing too. She didn't like that as much, but then again it usually paid a lot better.

At first, she didn't hear it, she was so engrossed in her work. Finally, the ringing of her cell cut through her concentration. Chloe's smiling face popped up, and she answered without a second thought.

"Hey, what's up?"

"I'll tell you what's up." Fuck. It couldn't be. How? Was he at Chloe's house? Had he hurt her, or the babies?

"What do you want, asshole."

"Brave, huh? You won't be for long once I get my hands on you."

"You better not have hurt her. I'll kill you myself."

"She's fine, for now. But don't push your luck. Meet me at the Fitness Center in ten minutes. If you're late one of the kids will die."

"I'll be there." She didn't have time to think, or even tell Alex. Chase's office was further than ten minutes away and she didn't have a car. How the hell was she supposed to get there?

Her guardian angel, fairy godmother, or someone wonderful must have been listening. Another man mountain knocked on the door and came to check to see if she needed anything. When she said a ride, he tossed her his keys. Chase had forgotten to put her on lockdown. Thank God. She left the laptop but grabbed her phone and purse and was out the door without a second thought. No way would Chloe suffer because of her. If he harmed one hair on her or any of the kid's heads, she would kill him.

In the parking garage, she clicked the unlock button and was thrilled when a black Lexus RC's lights flashed. She'd hit the jackpot. Hopefully, she didn't wreck it on the way. She climbed in and was out of there without a second thought. She had seven minutes to get to the Fitness Center.

Making it to there in six minutes really did make her think she had a fairy godmother. It should have taken at least twenty, but somehow there was no traffic, and she made every light. "Whoever you are, thank you. Now show me where Chloe and the kids are, pretty please?"

Parking at the back, as the voice instructed, she got out and made her way into the vacant, unfinished building. The first time she'd walked through the doors she'd been full of excitement. The thrill of new possibilities. This time only dread rode on her shoulders. As she walked toward the back offices, she looked around. It was almost ready for the finishing touches and staging. It would have been a great addition to the town. But she had her doubts that it would ever happen now.

Hopefully, it wouldn't turn into her final resting place. Thinking about it, made her wish she'd had one more kiss from Alex before she left. There was a very real possibility she'd never see him again. Her only chance was for him to track her phone. She'd kept it on and in her pocket, and if his computer skills were as good as he implied it should be enough. It was the only 'breadcrumb' she could leave.

The building was eerily quiet as she made her way into the administration area. He was waiting for her as she entered the back hallway. She didn't recognize him at all. Who the fuck was he, and where were Chloe and the kids?

"Where are they, you motherfucker. If you hurt them…"

"Relax, bitch. As much as I'd have enjoyed gutting the noisy brats, they're fine. I cloned her phone. They were never here. But you are, and no one is going to be able to help you."

Sheer relief filled Lily before she realized

what a mess she'd gotten herself into. Now she had to pray that Alex would be able to figure out where she was. In the meantime, she had to hold on, stay alive, until her Ranger could rescue his damsel in distress.

"Why are you doing this?"

"You can thank Walcott. He knew better than to hire you. We had a deal. He blew it off. Chandler knew better, too. But Walcott wouldn't listen. We needed to launder the money through the design company. At least until the fitness center opened. The drugs were coming in faster than we could handle it."

"This is over drugs and money? I don't get it. I'm a design firm."

"Yeah, but not ours, which was our front. Walcott decided to double cross us. He was out of his fucking mind. Sonny took care of him and the stupid bitch who worked for him. She squealed like a pig when we gutted her."

"Why did you have to kill her? What did she do to deserve that?"

"Bitch, in my world I decided who lives and dies, and I don't need a reason for either. She got in our way. Threatened to go to the police when she figured out what we were doing. Chandler was easy. He was all about the money, but Walcott was harder. We took his brother and had to send him a few fingers before he'd cooperate."

"So why did he bring me into all of this?"

"Beats the fuck out of me. Maybe he was hoping you'd figure something out and help expose it to get him off the hook. Who the hell knows. But it's too late for him too. No one will ever find him, he was a good meal for a few sharks the other day."

The blood drained from Lily's head, and if he hadn't been dragging her across the room, she'd have fallen. How could he be so cruel? She'd never met anyone who was such pure evil and all for money.

"What are you going to do with me?"

"I told you, you're next, bitch."

"What if I just walk away. I don't know who you are. I'll drop the project. You can do whatever you want."

"It doesn't work that way. I already to what I want. You caused me enough trouble. Now I need to see your blood run down my hands. I earned it."

He was a fucking serial killer who used money and drugs as motivation? How fucked up was that?

At least her phone was still in her pocket. She had no idea how long before Alex would realize she was gone, but she didn't think she had much time left. Once he did, he might be too late. At least Chloe and the kids were okay. She'd wrap her heart around that happy thought and hold on to it while he did whatever he was going to do.

She vowed if she made it out of this she was going to make Alex take her to the range so she could learn to shoot and get a conceal carry permit. No way would she allow herself to be defenseless ever again.

※ ※ ※

"Where the hell did she go? And how the fuck did she get out of here? She didn't even have a car." Alex was livid and terrified. Had they somehow managed to get their hands on his wife? The image of Enid on the video chilled him to his core. He would not let that happen to Lily.

"I don't know, but we have security cameras everywhere, it'll be easy enough to find out."

"Why weren't they on in the command center?"

"I didn't think we needed to monitor her every move. She was so shell-shocked I didn't think she'd even use the restroom."

"You don't know Lily. But still, for her to leave they must have used something as bait. She's not stupid and wouldn't have just taken off for no reason."

Chase called Rock and told him to pull up the feed for the conference room. He reported back that Colin had given her his keys and she'd left in his car about fifteen minutes earlier.

"Fuck. Does his car have tracking?"

"Probably, but what about her phone?"

"Duh." They headed back to the computers and Alex found her. "She's at the Fitness Center Complex. Her phone is still on at least."

"C'mon let's go. I'll have some of the guys come with us. I haven't heard from Steele so he must still be working the Enid issue."

Alex didn't need to be told twice. He wheeled faster than he thought possible, and Hunter kept neck and neck with him. He prayed they'd be in time. Why had she gone there? What could they have said? She knew he was safe in the building. Then he had a horrible thought. He called Logan.

"How are things going? I heard about the tires this morning."

"You have no idea. But I don't have time now. Do you know where your wife and kids are?"

"Yeah. Right here, I'm looking right at them. Why?"

"Just checking. I had a hunch, but maybe I was wrong. Do me a favor?"

"Sure."

"Don't let them out of your sight until I get back to you. And I mean not at all, for no reason anyone gives you except me. Got it?"

"Yeah I've got it. But you can't just say shit like that and not tell me what the fuck is going on."

"The Walcott thing blew up bigtime. Lily is missing. If you're smart, you won't tell Chloe because it will make keeping her in your sight a lot harder."

A low whistle was the response he got. "If you need me, or anything, you call, bro. I mean it."

"I will. I'll fill you in when I can." Alex clicked off without waiting for Logan's response. If Chloe was at home, why would Lily have left? He couldn't imagine anyone else she was close enough to for her to go into rescue mode.

The three SUVs from ESP arrived one after the other at the Fitness Center. Colin's car was parked around back, but there weren't any others in sight. Her phone was still on. She was inside. Or her phone was. But he refused to think about any other possibility except rescuing the love of his life. How much time had he wasted being bitter about his predicament? Yeah, he'd had pain and couldn't do what he wanted, but losing her would be so much worse. How would he survive if his heart died?

Chase and the guys hopped out of the car, while he had to wait for help with the wheelchair. He was beyond over this. He needed to get his ass in there and save his wife.

"Alex, you need to stay out here. You'll only be in the way. I'm sorry. But you need to let us do our jobs."

"No fuckin' way am I staying out here while you rescue Lily. You're out of your mind for even suggesting it." He looked up to see Rock trying to hide his smile. Damn straight. What man worth anything would stand by and let someone else rescue his wife? No one he fucking knew, that's for sure.

"You'll need to keep up. If you lag behind no one will wait with you."

"Fine. Now give me a piece so I can blow the fucker's brains out."

Chase handed him a Glock 19. "Coms off. We're going in silent."

Alex grabbed Hunter's leash and followed the SEALs into the building, praying his wife would be in one piece.

The only sound was Hunter's panting as they worked their way through the building. He hoped they wouldn't run into anything he couldn't navigate with the chair. He'd crawl to Lily if he had to. That gave him an idea

"Hunter, go find Lily." The dog looked at him as Alex unhooked his service vest. As soon as he had it off, Hunter bolted.

"Where the fuck is that dog going?"

"To find my wife. He'll get there a hell of a lot faster than we will."

"You're crazy."

"Maybe. But if there's a way to save her, I'm willing to do it."

They kept on their path. It wasn't long until

Hunter found his prey. A blood curdling scream, then another that was definitely Lily, was followed by the sound of a gunshot and a yelp. Alex couldn't get to his wife fast enough. His heart was beating double time as he imagined the worst-case scenario.

CHAPTER 12

After dragging her into the warehouse area, he'd hooked her to a hook on the wall. What the fuck was a huge hook doing on the wall anyway? Insurance would have fun with that one. Sorry, Mr. Walcott we can't approve you for your business insurance, you have medieval torture devices embedded in your walls. There went her inner dialogue again, she was really losing it. Helpless with a murderous madman and she's worried about hooks on the wall?

He'd tied her wrists together with rope, then looped them over the hook. Her feet barely reached the floor, and her shoulders were pulled so tight she knew it wouldn't take much to dislocate them. It probably wouldn't matter, though, she doubted she'd live to worry about it.

A nasty looking blade was laying on the table, and she cringed when he reached for it. He saw, and it made him smile even wider. Oh yeah, he was going to enjoy gutting her. Gut me, gut me, gut me. The words were dancing in her brain. What the fuck? Lily, you need to use your brain for good, girl, not ridiculousness. It's in there somewhere. How she wished she was better at gymnastics, she could have flipped herself off the hook. But nope, her chubby butt was sedentary, and up until now, she was perfectly happy with that.

"You don't have to do this. I swear I won't tell anyone." Now she sounded like every B movie heroine ever. Of course, he wasn't going to buy that. She was right too, all he did was laugh as he held up the knife, the blade catching the light and momentarily blinding her.

"I'm really going to like this. I hope you're a screamer. It's always better when they scream."

"Seriously? How fuckin' sick are you, asshole? How many people have you killed?"

That stopped him for a moment. He brought the knife point to his chin as he thought about it. Oh, to be able to high kick that fucker right into his chin would be perfect. Again, she wasn't Lara Croft or even Suzy Homemaker. No super defensive skills here.

"It'll be twenty after I'm done with you. Hopefully, I'll hit twenty-five before the end of the year. It'll match my age."

He's only twenty-five? He seemed much older, must be the evil running through his veins. Who was he and why was he in their little town? Again, Lily, not the time to be worrying about this.

He reached out and sliced open the front of her shit. She had a flashback to the video with Enid tied to the chair, her clothes sliced open and her chest filled with stab wounds. Fuck. This was going to hurt. As she prayed that Alex would get there before she was dead so she could tell him she loved him one more time, she heard a woof. Was it her imagination? It sure as hell sounded like Hunter.

Her view was blocked by the fucktard in front of her, but she heard him loud and clear when he growled again. He'd jumped onto the fucktard, knocking him into her. The knife he'd been holding went deep into her shoulder before he and Hunter felt to the ground. It hurt like hell. Would it be a life-threatening blow? She didn't think so. Thank you, thank you, thank you.

Hunter stood over the screaming man and went for his neck. The fucker screamed loud enough to wake the dead as the dog ripped open this throat. Blood gushed all over the dog and the piece of shit. She couldn't believe it, Alex's therapy dog was a damsel rescuing, evil killing super dog. Oh my God, she'd love him forever if they got out of this alive. Hell, even if they didn't.

She didn't see the gun until it was too late. The fucktard must have had one hidden under his shirt, and he pulled it out and shot Hunter. She screamed as Hunter yelped and fell to the floor.

"If you killed that dog I'm going to haunt you for the rest of your life. You piece of shit asshole fucktard douchenozzle." The stream of obscenities poured from her mouth as the blood poured from her shoulder where the knife was still embedded. Tears poured from her eyes as Hunter lay on the floor, whimpering.

The room was starting to spin when she thought she saw Alex in the doorway. She'd check in a minute. She just needed to close her eyes and rest. Just for a few minutes.

༄༅༄༅༄༅

He didn't know how he did it, but he and Chase made it there at the same time. Passing through the doorway and seeing the bloodbath inside the room almost stopped his heart. Lily hung from the wall by her arms, and his dog was in a pool of blood on the floor. The fucker that had caused it all was scooting across the floor, holding a hand over his throat, blood spurting from between his fingers, as he tried to get to his gun. But he never got the chance to touch it, both he and Chase pulled out their Glocks, and that was the end of him.

Now that the immediate danger was over, he rushed to Lily's side. She was unconscious, blood pouring from her wounded shoulder. He wanted to pull out the knife but was afraid she might bleed out.

Chase was on the phone calling for an ambulance. The other SEALs picked up Hunter while Chase unhooked Lily's arms. Alex had him put her across his lap, and he wheeled out of there. All the while he whispering to her. "Please baby, don't leave me. You have to live. Fight it, baby, you make me a good man. I need you, I want you. But most of all I love you.

The ambulances got there fast, but it still seemed like forever for Alex as Lily lay pale and bleeding in his arms. One took Lily to the hospital, and they convinced the other one to drop Hunter off at the animal hospital. It was good living in a small town sometimes. He'd wanted to go with her, but there was no room in the ambulance for him in the wheelchair.

"It's okay, I'll get you there. You know, that's some dog you got there. I hope he pulls through," Chase said as he followed the ambulance to the Willow Haven Hospital. Lily was a civilian so she couldn't go the military hospital.

"So do I, so do I."

When they got to the hospital, Lily was already in surgery. Alex had called Logan on the way there, and it wasn't long before he and Chloe, and the kids all piled into the waiting room with him. Chase and a few of the other SEALs hung around too.

"What the fuck is taking so long?"

"Dude, she lost a lot of blood. She'll be fine. Like you said, she's one tough woman."

Alex mumbled under his breath, "hopefully tough enough."

Soon the waiting room was filled with not only the guys from ESP but Tag, Julie, Mac, and Beth. He was struggling to hold it together when the surgeon came in.

"Which one of you is Mr. Barrett?"

"I am."

The doctor approached him, then kneeled, so she was eye level. "I'm Dr. Lambert. Your wife lost a lot of blood, and we had to give her two pints of blood, but she should make a full recovery. It may take a while before she has full use of her right arm, though."

"Thank you, doctor. Thank you." The tears he'd been holding onto for the last hour slid down his cheeks. She was going to be okay. He said it over and over like a mantra. Then turned to the others, who were anxiously awaiting the news.

"She's okay, she's going to make a full recovery." The mood in the room instantly changed, and there was a lot of back slapping and smack talking. Eventually, everyone left but Chloe. Logan took the kids home so she could stay with him.

"Thank you for staying."

"There's no way you were getting rid of me. She might as well be my sister. I'm just so thankful she'll be okay. You both will, right?"

He knew it was her way of making sure he was going to do right by Lily. "You better believe it."

EPILOGUE

Alex didn't get to talk to Lily until the next morning. She was heavily sedated and slept like the dead. It was scary, but the doctor said she'd be okay, and he was holding on to that. He sat with her, holding her hand and telling her his dreams for their future.

His cell rang. It was the Animal Hospital. Dreading the news, he answered the call. The doctor got right to the point, the bullet had missed anything major, and Hunter would pull through as well. After letting him know he'd be by to check on him as soon as he could, he thanked him and hung up.

"Thank you, God. I know I'm a sorry fucker, but you did me a solid and I'll be eternally grateful."

"Seriously? Is that how you pray?" Lily asked.

"How long have you been awake?"

"About a half an hour. I enjoyed listening to you tell me everything we're going to do. You do know how much I love you, right?

"Yes, Lilybee, but not nearly as much as I love you. If I'd lost you, the sun would never have risen again."

"I guess it's a good thing you don't have to worry about that, then, huh?"

"You know it. Now you need to hurry up and get better so we can start making those babies."

"I plan on it. How is Hunter?"

"He's going to be fine."

"I'm so glad. That dog is a superhero. He's getting anything he ever wants."

"He's a dog. I don't think he'll have a long list."

"I'll make one for him!"

"I need to thank Chase, too. Will he be around?"

"He had to leave town. He got a rush assignment in San Diego. But you can thank him when he gets back."

"Aren't you going to ask why I went there?"

"I already know. The fucker cloned Chloe's phone, and you thought he had her and the kids, right?"

"Yeah. How did you figure that out?"

"Wicked cool computer skills, remember? Okay, the crime scene techs found his phone. It was easy to figure out after that."

"I'm afraid to ask, did he make it?"

"No. You'll never have to worry about him again. But I swear, if you ever take off like that I'll paddle your butt when I find you, even if you are a bloody mess."

"Hmm, you never know, I might like it." She stuck her tongue out. But the surprise was on her when he stood up and leaned over the bed, taking her lips in a kiss meant to curl her toes.

"You work miracles, Lilybee. See, I told you."

"I love you, Alex. Thank you for coming back to me."

If you liked this book or any other, please consider leaving a written review on your retailer of choice. It really helps your favorite authors! Lynne xoxo

ABOUT THE AUTHOR

Lynne St. James is the author of over seventeen books in paranormal, new adult, and contemporary romance. She lives in the mostly sunny state of Florida with her husband, an eighty-five-pound fluffy Dalmatian-mutt horse-dog, a small Yorkie-poo, and a cat named Pumpkin who rules them all.

When Lynne's not writing stories about second chances and conquering adversity with happily-ever-afters, you'll find her with a mug of coffee, a crochet hook, or a book (or e-reader) in her hand.

Where to find Lynne:

Email: lynne@lynnestjames.com

Website: http://lynnestjames.com

VIP Newsletter sign-up: http://eepurl.com/bT99Fj

- facebook.com/authorLynneStJames
- twitter.com/lynnestjames
- instagram.com/lynnestjames
- amazon.com/Lynne-St.James
- bookbub.com/profile/lynne-st-james

BOOKS BY LYNNE ST. JAMES

Beyond Valor Series

A Soldier's Gift, Book 1

A Soldier's Forever (*Previously A Soldier's Surprise*), Book 2

A Soldier's Triumph, Book 3 – ESP Agency Novel

A Soldier's Protection (*Previously Protecting Faith*), Book 4 – (re-release soon)

A Soldier's Pledge, Book 5 – ESP Agency Novel

A Soldier's Destiny (*Previously Guarding Aurora*), Book 6 – (re-release soon)

A Soldier's Temptation (*Previously Protecting Ariana*), Book 7 – (re-release soon)

A Soldier's Homecoming, Book 8 – ESP Agency Novel (coming soon)

A Soldier's Redemption, Book 9 – ESP Agency Novel (coming Soon)

Raining Chaos Series

Taming Chaos, Book 1

Seducing Wrath, Book 2

Music under the Mistletoe, Book 2.5 – A Raining Chaos Christmas (Novella)

Tempting Flame, Book 3

Anamchara Series

Embracing Her Desires, Book 1

Embracing Her Surrender, Book 2

Embracing Her Love, Book 3

The Vampires of Eternity Series

Twice Bitten Not Shy, Book 1

Twice Bitten to Paradise, Book 2

Twice Bitten and Bewitched, Book 3

Made in the USA
Monee, IL
06 March 2020